# DUETS

First published in 2024
by Scratch Books Ltd
London

Jacket design © Alice Haworth-Booth, 2024
Original cover image: McGill Library
Typesetting by Will Dady, 2024

ISBN 9781739830168

Printed on FSC-accredited paper in the UK by 4edge Limited

# Contents

# Introduction

This is a book of stories, each written by two people. After the *Reverse Engineering* series, I wanted to commission stories that made a feature of their craft, where the drama of their writing is palpable in our reading them.

When introducing the project to the authors, I suggested they send the work back and forth, as though weaving the story between them. However – as they set out in their notes at the back of the book – the methods they came to use were more inventive and challenging, giving their stories greater scope for correspondence, greater richness and, yes, a greater drama.

Tom Conaghan
Scratch Books

# Merrily Merrily Merrily Merrily

## Nell Stevens & Eley Williams

When I strip the wallpaper in the new flat, I find, underneath it, strange scratches in the plasterwork, lines and curves like an unknown alphabet, finger marks covering the wall behind my bed. I'm anxious to get rid of the wallpaper, though there are countless more urgent things; faced with the splintered floorboards and rotting window frames left behind by the previous owner, and a leaking pipe under the kitchen sink that drips into an old lemonade bottle, it seems easier to worry first about the bedroom walls. I have it in my head that if I can just replace the yellowed chintzy pattern with something calm, I too might feel calmer. If I can just get that done, everything else might feel more manageable.

But now there are the marks, which could perhaps be nothing, maybe something to do with the way the wallpaper glue dried, but which seem intentionally communicative somehow, ubiquitous and affronting. I do not feel calm at all, even when I cover the walls with fresh plasterboard and then with blue-green-grey paint from an expensive paint company.

I sense the scratches underneath, lingering and emphatic. I convince myself I can still see them, despite everything.

I practise saying, 'this is home,' as I move around the space. The dog runs from room to room, tail wagging so furiously his whole body bends into parentheses, sniffing out histories in corners, catching cobwebs on the wet of his nose. I order takeaway – which I eat sitting on boxes of unpacked crockery – and buy sourdough from the bakery at the bottom of the road, crust serrated against my hard palate. In the garden, I assemble a wooden table and chairs amongst overgrown, straggly rose plants that should have been pruned years ago and, having not been, now seem untouchable.

'This is home,' I say to the roses.

'This is home,' I say to the boiler, whose buttons and dials I am too scared to adjust.

It is natural enough to feel uneasy, I think. Everything is so new. Natural enough not to want to sleep beneath a wall covered in half-realised hieroglyphics, to find my changed circumstances, my sudden aloneness, unsettling. I fill bin liners with sheathes of torn-off wallpaper and vacuum the previous owner's strange dust. There are ball bearings wedged between the floorboards in the hallway, an invoice from a vet taped to the inside of one of the kitchen cupboards. An eyelash curler, rusting, like a historic torture device in the dungeon of the basement bathroom. Soon, this unfamiliar rubbish will be replaced by my own rubbish, I tell myself, and I will feel calm again.

~

She has narrated me without knowing it, so perhaps it is not entirely rude to return the favour in kind. Right now she is holding a half-finished box of cornflakes and standing in the centre of the new-to-her kitchen, pivoting on the spot and pondering where best to commit to storing cereal. It says something about her, doesn't it, that she thought it was worth packing a half-finished box of cornflakes when moving house. It certainly says something about me that I choose to dwell on this detail about her. I watch her trial the cornflakes on different heights of shelves and in different cupboards. She is talking to herself throughout this process, about the most humane way to trap moths. She had the same muttered monologue yesterday and plainly did not come to a resolution. Watching her, I have learned that she sings to herself sometimes too, but never seems to complete a tune. I wonder whether she knows that about herself, or is it entirely thoughtless? When I am able to recognise the lyrics, I pitch in and finish the songs as her own voice trails away – that is, when her interest in sustaining the song trails off, or her memory of its words trails off, or something better dislodges the song from her mind. *On a bicycle made for two*, I sing, once she's finished with her *Daisy*s as she is scrubbing the bathroom floor; *Crying 'Cockles and mussels, alive, alive-o!'*, I add while she's respooling the vacuum cleaner's cable, having given up on her *Molly Malone*; at the end of a particularly dispirited rendition of half of *Row Row Row Your Boat*, I trill the final cheery *Life is but a dream*. She cannot hear me, naturally – or otherwise – but I notice that her dog wags his tail in something like recognition. The

11

tap-swish of his tail against the floor disturbs the dust. I bend to pat the air above her dog, stirring it with my fingertips, and watch as he ducks a little, his happy tail at odds with the twinge of confusion creeping about his tongue-lolling face.

*A dream*, I sing again, refinishing the unfinished song to nobody. As she keeps working on the house, sweating a little, making private whinnying breaths of exertion and satisfaction, I think about why I feel compelled to supply any song's end. For my own amusement? To imagine we are in a company, in a chorus? I suppose I can't bear on some level to have anything else left hanging in the air, not even a nursery rhyme.

I speculate about her life, the fact that so many of the half-sung songs she knows are from childhood. Hers, or some others?

She has a good voice. I wonder whether anybody knows that about her, or maybe she only sings to herself when she thinks that she's alone.

~

I wake up expecting someone to be here. I imagine my name is being called, that I am being summoned to tie shoelaces, to scramble eggs, that I am about to rush headlong into a morning full of school bags and spilled drinks and late-for-the-bus-can-you-give-me-a-lifts. How long has it been since anyone needed me to tie their shoelaces? And yet, still, that is what the silence suggests to me, and I jump up from bed and start towards the door before I realise, no, no, nobody needs me.

12

The dog's claws on the floorboards. His paw against the back door, asking to be let out. His breath, ragged in my ear. The click of his tongue in his mouth when he pants. Sometimes he barks at nothing at all and I love it and wish he'd do it more, wish he'd startle me or be more unexpected, because one of the things, one of the most weighty, alarming things about my life now, is the feeling that I am the only thing that can change other things. But he is a creature of strong rhythms, and once he has overcome the shock of his new environs, he reverts to predictability. Kibble between his teeth. His tail thumping against my leg. The way that, when he drinks water from the bowl, the sound is somehow crunchy and small droplets scatter across the tiles.

I try out different ways of living in silence. First: drowning it out with radio dramas, or by playing true crime Netflix shows on my laptop, but I sense the quiet of the flat beneath the ominous sound effects and the voiceovers. It is like sweeping dust under a rug: the silence is still there, lurking. Next I try to expand into it, dragging my feet across the floorboards to make a louder shuffle than is necessary. Coughing, clearing my throat as though about to make a speech. And then, with increasing frequency, what happens is that I sing. I sing whatever I can think of, though I can never think of much more than the opening lines of things: nursery rhymes, silly childhood ditties, national anthems (British, American, and my favourite, French). The dog watches me sceptically, cocking his head to one side, half-whining and then, without warning, urinating in the middle of the floor of what is going to be my study, which is absolutely not the kind of startling thing I'd wanted him to do.

*Row, row, row your boat*, I sing, as I mop and disinfect. *Gently down the stream.*

When I look up I notice there are orange damp stains on the ceiling, blossoming across the white paintwork like flowers, and for a moment I feel as though everything is upside down, as though what I am looking at is not the ceiling but the patch where the dog pissed on the floor, and I am suspended above my life, detached from it all, and nothing makes sense anymore. It was not supposed to look like this, I think. Where has everyone gone? Where have I gone?

~

I introduce myself to the dog when her back is turned and she is stripping the wallpaper in the bedroom. In my limited experience and according to my limited observation, dogs can usually smell the difference when I'm in a room. As evidenced by his reaction to my singing, it seems clear that dogs can hear me, or detect some rearrangement of air or pressure in a way that is similar to hearing. Letting the dog *see* me might be fairer on this sweet little spaniel – allow him to know that I am keeping his mistress company. It feels cruel otherwise to let him catch drifts of me in this piecemeal way, scurrying with his nose pressed to the skirting boards and wainscotting with such a busy and bemused expression, as he tracks me from room to room without seeing anyone there. No need for fruitless snuffle-inquisition, little one.

*Here I am*, I say, and I reveal myself to the dog. We are in the doorway of what used to be my parlour, but since my time in this house came to its own kind of end it has since been used as a dressing room, a bachelor's room, a guest room, a child's (*Merrily merrily merrily merrily, life is but a dream!*) playroom, a bedroom once more. Now she plans to use it as a 'study'. Hence all the books. I approve; a study is a good choice for a room with these dimensions and aspect. There is excellent light there in the evenings. I used to look out from its window, down at my garden as it was. I used to dream about the roses I could plant there one day. She might have the same idea; we might share something in that way.

The dog does not take well to seeing me. He relieves himself and runs from the room and I vanish, embarrassed, and will feel guilty for weeks. I must force myself not to stroke his ears in apology, to keep my distance so he is not too alarmed. I stop singing the end of the new homeowner's abandoned sentences in case the disembodied sound of it causes him distress.

~

I bought the flat and moved in within a month of first viewing it. The previous owner was anxious to sell, the estate agent said, without giving me a reason why, and I said I was anxious to buy, without giving a reason why either.

The place is, compared to others I viewed, large, the ground floor of an austere-looking Victorian house: a bedroom, open-plan kitchen-living room and a smaller reception room with doors that open out onto a scrappy back garden. The smaller room, I imagine, will be my study. The bathroom is downstairs in the basement and smells damp. Walking around on that first visit, the estate agent said, 'I can really see you living here,' which was reassuring, as though in some alternate world I was already living here, as though the decision was already made and all I had to do was simply succumb to it. 'Garden could be nice,' he said, 'with a little sprucing up. South-facing.' The garden is west-facing but I didn't correct him.

He stepped out to take a phone call, and I heard him saying, 'I'm just with a lady at Mayfield Road. Yes. Yes, keen. No, alone. Yes.'

Later that same day, I emailed an offer at the top of my budget, considerably below the asking price, and was a bit alarmed to get a call, minutes later, saying it had been accepted. How quickly could I proceed, they wanted to know. I told them I could proceed quickly.

~

There are parallels between us in many ways, of course. If I revealed myself to her, maybe it's such things that we have in common that might form a basis for any kind of understanding? Woman to once-woman? Homeowner to previous tenant; dust to dust. I find it useful to think of myself as the dust itself, sometimes. Why would that be? Better to be a sweepable presence than an inhabited absence? Moted and moping and unmopped in the corners. Maybe it's comforting to think that people, alive and vivid and blundering and beat-hearted are pre-dust. Maybe it is comforting to think that I might swirl.

To think dust could ever be so fanciful.

~

People tried not to look shocked when I told them about the move; they smiled and nodded and said how invigorating it would be to have a change. Nobody said anything tactless, though I knew they were thinking tactless things. *I suppose you don't need all that space anymore. Well, at least you've got the dog for company.* I try to frame it as a good thing. A new phase of life. I'd have a little study, somewhere to keep my books. Perhaps I'd finally have a chance to read them all.

And it's true that it feels momentous, it does, as I layer on coats of new paint, as I run cloths along skirting boards rippled with grime, as I watch a YouTube video explaining how to turn on this particular kind of oven. It is momentous to commit, fixedly and determinedly, to being alone – to being so alone that I have bought a place for nobody other than me to live in. What was the word I feel tempted to use? Empowering. I can't quite bring myself to use it. I stack the books in piles against the walls, where they tilt, teeter, threaten to fall.

Because I am as shocked as anyone else to find myself here. To have lived, it turns out, many lives in this one life: to have shared houses with parents, with friends, with partners, with children, and now to find myself nonetheless alone, with nobody to bear witness to whatever comes next. I did not foresee that it would be like this, somehow, did not anticipate aloneness; I spent so long not being alone it seemed impossible that might ever change. Waking up thinking: oh, they need me, and now waking up thinking: oh, there is nobody here.

17

I buy cheap shelves and begin the process of organising the books. I start, ambitious, alphabetising, singing the ABC song – *won't you sing along with me?* – and then, quite quickly, give up and settle for genres: poetry, plays, children's, non-fiction, fiction. The air in the boxes smells like my old house when I open them, my old life and the people who used to live in it with me. Sometimes, when I slide a book out, it throws up a little splutter of dust. I breathe it in, and out, and in again, and it mixes with the air of the new flat.

'This is home,' I say, to the dog.

'This is home,' I say, to the air between me and the doorway.

'This is home,' I say, to the dust.

~

She is coughing a little now, and rubbing her eyes. I inch closer, concerned for her but also thrilled to see a body doing what it does best, what I did once: reacting without conscious effort, without consciousness.

She is looking something up on her phone. How pleasing – I see she is reading about dust; we are clearly on the same wavelength. She reads aloud to her dog what is on her screen.

'Dead skin cells, dust mites, dead insect particles, soil, pollen, tiny plastic particles, bacteria, hair—' she lists. She looks satisfied by this explanation.

I've no right to, but I am affronted, to have someone claim they can know anything about dust in this way. Such certainty about so uncertain a presence. I point at the bookshelves lining the room around us (*Isn't it interesting that one of the first things she unpacked was all these boxes of books? I remember thinking. I read all the poetry there in a single glance last night as she slept, and committed all their pages to memory*) and draw up right alongside her.

*I will show you fear in a handful of dust*, I imagine intoning.

*For everything exists and not one sigh nor smile nor tear, one hair nor particle of dust, not one can pass away*! I imagine hissing by her pillow that night, glowering through the gloom.

The dog's ears twitch.

Or some Shelley, a personal favourite of mine. *Methought*, I imagine quoting loftily at her some future July evening, settling quite quite close to her ear as I might lean forward and break our companionable silence, daring my breath to meet her cheek to read, *I sate beside a public way thick strewn with summer dust...*

She swats at the side of her head as if annoyed by a fly and coughs again. For his part, the dog is looking right through me and softly brewing a bark in his throat.

'What's up?' she asks him, tenderly.

I withdraw to the shadows of the wall.

'Gently down the stream—' she sings beneath her breath, giving the dog's head a fondle, and I press something like my back against and through the wall amongst my mites and particles once more, biding something like time, *merrily merrily merrily merrily.*

# Keep Your Miracles to Yourself

Zoe Gilbert & Jarred McGinnis

I leaned over the railing, looking into the green glass of the canal's water. A mobility scooter and a traffic cone, monotoned by a layer of muck, lay at the bottom like Pompeii lovers. Beautiful and gross in the way only cities manage honestly.

The decision to walk was partly to delay the moment that I would have to tell my wife, Jo, bobbing and cradling our first and newly born child, that I had been fired. A point five yearly contract lecturing twentieth century visual design was no prize but I had little else to offer my family. Bad luck, not my fault. Last to be hired; first to be fired. Adding the stupidity of leaving the car on campus wasn't going to help things, but I needed to think and clarity does not come to those stuck in traffic behind a white van with 'I wish my wife was this dirty' scrawled in road grime. So, I took a walk.

I held the submarine shadows of cone and scooter in my sight and in my mind with a knuckle-white fierceness. When thoughts – we're already hurting for money – crooked their dirty fingers through a gap in my attention, I stared harder at their forms. Neither my family nor hers were in a position to help out. The fur of algae smoothed out the shape of the chewed-up scooter until it was close to elegant, as if someone had armed a palinka-ravaged Brâncuşi with a flocking gun. The traffic cone was simple to begin with, laid there resting its tip on the back wheel of the scooter. A hopeful sort of moment. I could shuffle some of the balances between credit cards, maybe see if I could still get one of those 0% introductory rate cards. Maybe I don't tell her anything. Stupid idea. I couldn't bear it. A secret like that would eat through my insides. My wife can handle worry. What was troubling me was how quickly she would shoulder my problem. She'll deny herself her weekly manicure, her one indulgence, too readily.

The truth of it is that before my son – Danny – was born, getting sacked *would* have been my fault. The loneliness of this island and the grey, always grey, had seeped into the marrow of me, and the drinking had gone long past fun. When he arrived, he did so without a peep. As they held him up to me, he looked around to see the hand fate had dealt him; he seemed unimpressed. The swaddle was blood-flecked from where they pulled him from the sunroof of my wife. She was out cold from the long labour followed by an emergency caesarean. We locked eyes and I felt a nothing so complete that I turned and walked out of the hospital. I could no longer be the me I was. With each step, hour upon hour, meeting after meeting, the I of me spilled out and trailed behind me until the next morning, I followed the line of dust

22

I had left back to where my wife and son lay. I handed her a white poker chip.

'I was starting to wonder where you were,' she said, examining the poker chip. 'Do you want to say hello to Danny?'

I put my hand on the sleeping bundle, tiny but immense, at her chest.

'They give you this poker chip when you are sober for one day,' I said. 'That one there is yours, as my promise. Next meeting, I'll get one for myself.' That was all I said and we cried together.

I was surprised to find I had slumped to the ground, my back against the railing. The scooter and its traffic cone bride looked up at me unconcerned. Pigeons did their peck and bob a few feet away. One of the pigeons moved with a clockwork wobble on the withered black remnant of its foot. A sucker punch of grief hit me. I had tapped into a pure clean sadness. My soul had touched the die from which all sadnesses were cast. An unintentional prayer was made and it floated up uneasily. I felt the gaze of God turn to me. He cleared his throat and drew breath to answer.

There was a sound; a pop, or a slap, the wet clamour of the abattoir. The pigeons scattered in silent panic of wings except one. It was dead. Surprisingly bloodless, the organs had burst out of the empty canoe of its body. A streamer of intestine hung from the hole like an exhausted party horn. A vivid purple gizzard clung to the earthly clay of liver, a foot or two from the body. The dead eyes were as unreadable as they'd been in life. With my foot, I flipped the viscera back into its nest of ribs and dropped the errant liver into the beggar's bowl of a pigeon. I set her in the water to drift off – her own funeral barrique.

A pain in my stomach flashed chip-pan-fire fast and radiated out towards my back. I staggered and ran from the canal, collapsing against a stone abutment near the road, convinced some gun-nut had my number. I closed my eyes. Exhaled. And opened my eyes to see nothing. The pain was still there, bold as fox shit on a doorstep, but no blood. Save for the redness where my own hand had grabbed at my stomach, my flesh was unmarked and whole. I tried to calm myself, take stock of what had happened as the pain collapsed to a diamond-hard spot full of resentful agony. Under my hand a knot nuzzled beneath my flesh. I pushed it and something rolled inside me – a ripple of skin followed its wake and a new explosion of pain rattled the tin cans of my spine.

~

All they want is love. This was Cassandra's motto, a way to bring the team back to first principles when I or one of the other girls got carried away with our methods.

'Love,' she would remind us, tapping each of us on the head with her gold propeller-pencil, 'is many-splendoured. But here at Auricle, we make our Chosen Ones feel...?'

We would trot it out:

'Lucky.'

'Original.'

'Validated.'

'Exceptional.'

24

'Check your method,' she would say, clicking out a 3mm length of pencil lead and breaking it off with her perfect teeth, 'against the rubric. Which feeling will this act elicit? If it's none of the above, ditch it.' Then she would swallow and smile, eyes narrowed.

Cassandra, Auricle's top dog, taught me everything I know about reeling in the best Chosen Ones. The other girls on Team Cassie fledged early, bouncing off with what they believed were her secrets to rival firms like Genie or Nightingale. But I was her true protégée. I stayed on at Auricle and rose through the ranks, my list gaining rave reviews. Fifteen boxes of propeller-pencil refills later, I found Martin Sutch, and was finally ready to stage my coup. I had hoped the lead-nibbling would do the job for me but, it turns out, graphite is not toxic.

But I digress. L.O.V.E. is, ultimately, what our Chosen Ones must feel. Furthermore, everything, from the inciting incident onwards, must appear personal. It isn't, of course, but the illusion is essential, and the best sort of Chosen One is predisposed. They are not all narcissists (though we do like those) but ideally they already see themselves surrounded by meanings and metaphors exclusively explanatory of their own life-journey.

Martin Sutch was mine, my first solo find undertaken without Cassandra breathing graphite fumes down my neck. And what a beauty. I knew from the moment his wife started talking about him, her eyes glistening as our cuticles were oiled by masked salon minions. Yes, Martin Sutch would be the one to let me leapfrog Cassandra and put me top of the

Muse Board at Auricle. The nail bar had only been open a few weeks when I found it, clocked that it was still free of rival scouts. Nail bars were my very own innovation. Cassandra, being old-school, stuck to yoga retreats and high-end rehabs. But there's something about the manicure process, the intimacy of hunching fingertip by fingertip with minimal eye contact, that brings the gold to the surface quickly.

We don't tick boxes at Auricle, it's too reductive, but if we did, just look at his credentials: a poetic soul in pain; susceptible to symbolism; delusions of a communicating higher power; tendency to read deep meaning into inanimate objects; heightened emotional register. All I needed to add was pressure, a thumb pad on life's sternum.

Side by side, as our nails were glued and top-coated and buffed, the wife told me all about the poker chips, the new baby, the love. Really, it sounded quite romantic. His story was writing itself, but it was lacking in jeopardy. A single anonymous email to his boss sufficed. And from that moment on, intensive surveillance. Be present at the Event, and a Chosen One will fall into your palm like a lucky penny.

We don't know why the Event occurs. There is perhaps some disturbance or redistribution of energy at the point of the Chosen One's metaphysical enhancement. But it is, for us, both jubilant and extremely useful, indicating as it does that we have correctly identified a Chosen One. In this case I had been looking forward to it the way you might look forward to fireworks, or the popping of champagne corks (which it would surely presage), and when that pigeon goop squirted out onto the towpath, I could have crowed for joy.

I did not. I kept very quiet and still, crouched on the footbridge, because the Event is also vital for the Chosen One who is about to experience severe pain. For a certain type of person, the Event smooths the transition from basic crisis to physical metamorphosis. The Chosen One perceives the Event Vehicle (in this case, the pigeon) as the symbolic counterpart to the transformation of self that is about to occur. As an extra bonus in this case, having seen the innards of the bird, the Chosen One is relieved not to see his own. He may be in severe mental and physical distress, but at least he is not trailing viscera onto a filthy tow path.

But I am getting ahead of myself with all this theory, delicious as it is. Let us return to first principles. How does the Event, and the subsequent discomfort, make the Chosen One feel? Terrible. He likely believes he is dying. Swiftly, we must make him feel L.O.V.E. It may take a little longer to persuade him he is Lucky, but he is already Original; shortly his doomy slump into generalised grief will be Validated; and this peculiar experience, along with the glory that will follow, is what will make him Exceptional.

He was reeling, of course, bewildered horror in his wide-open eyes. This is the moment of highest risk, but also of greatest excitement. I hit send on a message to Pandora, confirming that Dr Liu should be put on standby for Severance, then I pelted off the bridge towards him. I could see the cogs whirring as he clutched his belly and gazed at me, stupefied. I threw my arms around him and we tumbled together. It was a beautiful moment.

Our offices are like any other. We don't do brand logos at Auricle, our business being irreducible to anything so tacky. I led my prize, staggering and groaning, directly to the Cosy. Before I personally directed the revamp, this room had been the headquarters of Team Cassie. Perhaps it was my heightened state, but despite the new abstract prints and shiny deco lighting, I thought I still caught a whiff of graphite. My waiting assistants, Thalia and Pandora, looked nervous, glancing down the corridor behind Martin. They had been sworn to secrecy, on pain of redundancy, lest Cassandra find out what was afoot and snatch glory from me. Perhaps I had underestimated the pressure they felt. Jeopardy! What a thrill. But I soon brought them to their senses with a meaningful glare. Poise is vital at this stage; the Chosen One must feel confident that we, too, see him as Exceptional, and trust that we will ease his pain. Pandora nodded to confirm Dr Liu was on site. Thalia took my cue, and reached out her shaking hands to support our Chosen One. I slid my palm across his belly. He gasped. I was one step closer to triumph.

~

'I wasn't shot?' I asked, taking in the operating theatre.

'No one's shot you, silly.' It was the lady who found me after I was shot, or not shot. 'You have a gift, Martin. We're going to bring this gift to the world, together.' She had these earrings like small chandeliers, which plinked and tinkled as she craned her neck. My wife, Jo, would have called them Statement Earrings.

'Has anyone called my wife?' I asked.

A white-haired woman in purple scrubs stepped close and asked from behind her mask, 'can we proceed?'

The woman nodded, earrings tinkling. She smiled beatifically at me then stepped away.

I didn't feel the cut of the scalpel. There was a chill of cold air felt inside me, a dribble of liquid down my side. But that was all. There was some pressure as the surgeon moved around inside me. One of the nurses stumbled back. The surgeon snatched away her gloved hands, pink-smeared as if she had been bitten. She was handed a silver instrument. I felt its tug inside me then there was a wet flatulent sound – like when Danny blows raspberries – at which everyone recoiled. It crescendoed to a kettle whistle before settling into something close to a mistlethrush's song. The surgeon barked for a clamp. The pain roiled and sped along my nerves, radiating from my abdomen. I shot up and two nurses threw their entire weight on me. Morphine was ordered and delivered but the pain only built. My vision blurred and alarms shrilled above the strangled melancholic notes coming from the incision. The surgeon withdrew the clamp and the pain stopped.

The woman's earrings chimed her arrival before she appeared at my bedside in the recovery room.

'Martin, you are a lucky man, twice-fold. You are lucky because fate, the universe, god-herself, sent me at the very moment you needed me most.' She paused, seemingly pleased with her pronouncement.

'I can't thank you enough for saving me and bringing me to the hospital. Is that where we are?'

She smiled and nodded, but said nothing more.

'Twice-fold?' I asked.

'Yes. Lucky twice because, Martin, what ails you has a name, and naming things is the first step to mastering them.' She lifted the sleeve of my hospital gown with a pen to examine my tattoo, a poorly drawn pair of jump wings done one drunken night during my time in the army. 'Are you ready to know the name of your tormentor, Martin?'

I nodded.

'Gerhwek. Shall we pronounce it together? Let it know that we hold power over it.'

We did – Gerhwek – like an amen at church. When she showed me black and white slices of salami that were the MRI of my guts, I asked if she was a doctor. She pointed out a snail-shell curl of bright white amongst the mishmash of grey.

'What feels like a painful burden now is actually something that makes you quite exceptional, Martin,' she said. 'Your… do you remember the word, Martin?'

'Gerhwek.'

'Good. I promise we tried all that we could, but your Gerhwek is inoperable. It would have been better for all concerned if we had achieved a Severance, but that is not our fate, I'm afraid.' She motioned toward my gown. 'Do you mind?' She rolled the gown up and adjusted my sheets. She delicately pulled back the tape and bandages so as not to pull or pinch my still tender skin. 'We took the unique decision to put in a port. We are a part of history, Martin.'

'Thank you so much. I've never felt pain like that. I thought I was—' Where my stomach used to be was a small round window, similar to a washing machine but, instead of my smalls rolling around in happy soapy suds, we stared at my digestive system thrumming and glistening.

'—going to die.'

We both leaned in to see peeking from underneath my stomach, and resting upon the gutty pillow of my lower intestines, a white mass of scar clinging to the surrounding organs. Upon this fibrous dais of tissue lay a perfect set of lips. So perfect that if they hadn't been attached to my internal organs, they would have had a career with Revlon.

Of course, I asked the immediate and vital question: 'what the fuck is it?'

'Ġerhwek, Martin. Shall we?' she asked, twisting the brass screw to open the window. A cool rush of air tickled parts I didn't know had nerves. The lips pursed then parted, blooming like a time-lapse flower. Its song issued from the porthole and reached out through the walls of the room to fraying edges of the universe. The poker chip in my pocket began to tap out a message to the one in my wife's purse, like the Morse code signals between two cheap walkie talkies.

I understood. I loved her.

I understood. I loved my boy. Our bond was a hazy field of wavy lines pulling me to him.

I understood. The lady standing there with a dreamy look and a tear sliding down her cheek didn't care about me. She saw the Ġerhwek as a thing, no matter what name she gave it. It didn't upset me to realise this. Though she felt the sadness of its song, it would just be a song to her. And that was okay too.

'Lovely.' She closed the window and twisted the brass down. 'The world will know us, Martin. We, you, will be famous. Oh yes.'

~

Oh yes, it was a blow. I admit that single tear was for myself, my great plan, the ousting of Cassandra from the top spot on the Auricle Muse Board. I was so angry, I might have had the surgeon's clamp tightened all the way, relished the gurgles and the long flatlining squeal that would have marked the end of Martin Sutch.

But there wouldn't have been any point. Cassandra once showed me the infamous Erlem Ġerhwek, which had shrivelled the moment it was sliced from Ernesto Erlem's gushing abdomen and, by the time he died in a pool of blood, resembled a spent balloon. She refused to play the recording of its song, but I found it in the archives and believe me, you don't want to go rooting around for it. Like a toddler parroting ad jingles, is all I'll say. Tragic, facile: everything Auricle is not.

So, Severance had not been an option. My genius, lost on Martin and most of the junior team at Auricle, was in the acquisition and insertion of the port – and in coming up with this innovation during an extraordinarily stressful episode. But the result was beyond all I could have hoped for.

While I gazed at Martin's Ġerhwek in its gently pulsing nest of innards, I recalled the morning I was first permitted into Cassandra's office. There were still four of us acolytes. In we shuffled, tugging at our pastel shift dresses and twisting our bracelets, excited to be granted entry to the inner sanctum. There on the marble mantelpiece stood eleven glass domes, their names and dates in gold on the bases. Within each dome, a unique anomaly: pairs of lips or sets of teeth; a wet, flickering tongue; a voice box held in a filigree cradle of cartilage like spun sugar. My favourite was the miniature head, with eyes and nose and cherubic mouth, though with no ears to spoil the olive smoothness of its virgin skin. With great ceremony, Cassie lifted the domes one by one. Now, I'm no writer, so my descriptions won't do their songs justice: chirrups, whistles, sonorous bass, tinkling laughter and theremin glissando – like a choir of crazy angels, or a psychedelic trip in sound.

After she replaced the final dome, Cassandra clicked out a full inch of lead from her gold propeller pencil and let it lie on her tongue. We were all in a state of bliss. For what we had just heard was the sound of our future success: the new Gerhweks we would discover, making Auricle the biggest and best, and each of us an industry name. There would be op-eds, prizes, OBEs. There would be Desert Island Discs.

I'm being surprisingly generous in my recollections of Cassandra, aren't I? But that's because not one of those Gerhweks, not even all eleven of them in combination, sang as beautifully as Martin's. And I believe it's down to the live circulation. His blood, that is. Infusions of red wine, extract of foie gras and nicotine, for example, had the results we would have expected. As we worked our way through stimulants, relaxants, alteratives and probiotics, Martin's pallor diminished. While the fidelity of his Ǵerhwek's tone improved with these tweaks, sadly, his resistance to our very necessary exploration did not.

Take the presentation to our CEO, Electra, last week. My first time in the Temple. Yet despite my jitters, Martin refused mild sedation, and howled quite rudely when Electra unscrewed the port window she had paid for out of Auricle's coffers and reached in for a quick caress. She didn't flinch. With her forefinger she depressed that bee-stung lower lip inside Martin, peered beyond, and in a trademark Electra move, leaned in for a kiss. It took all the tricks in my L.O.V.E. toolbox to calm him down back in the Cosy. Really I thought I'd be easing off on all that sweet talk by this stage. But he is certainly L-for-Lucky, because Electra's allocation for the Martin Sutch budget broke company records. Not that Martin can know this. Advertising is expensive and our team is large. But it's all so exciting! So exceptionally thrilling, in fact, that I couldn't resist showing off Auricle's first ever Hosted Ǵerhwek to Cassandra. And I'd say it went well, in that she stayed very quiet, circling Martin, pressing her gold pencil so far into her jacket pocket I could see its tip through the viscose. Martin rolled his eyes at her. I had visions of his Ǵerhwek choking on fine slivers of lead, but I kept my cool, thinking of that gargantuan budget. From my seat on the Temple steps I would look down upon Cassandra and her inferior detached Ǵerhweks.

'Why?' she asked me afterwards in the corridor.

I looked her up and down, pausing at her scrawny kneecaps, which I know she believes are her least attractive feature. 'Progress,' I said, as lightly as if observing the shift to reusable coffee cups. 'This is the future, Cassie. And it's mine.'

~

There's no good way to show your wife a mad woman in a power suit from Next has turned you into a human submarine.

'You didn't have to do this.'

I felt ashamed as I removed my shirt, button by button. I couldn't look at her standing before me with our boy at her breast. I turned the brasses but did not open the port.

'Martin!' she said, her free hand covering her mouth. Danny pulled away from feeding with a loud wet smack. I opened the port and its song poured thick as honey into our tiny living room. The shock and fear and anger drifted away as the song took her. She understood its importance and I knew we'd be okay. Baby Danny watched my face, not understanding where the music was coming from. The room dissolved into whiteness. He smiled and listened, drifting off to sleep. I felt proud as I closed the port and dropped my shirt. My wife laid him down gently and we shared a moment staring at our son. She held me; her head barely reached my chest and sobbed. I rubbed her back and told her it's alright; we'll be alright.

On the day of the big meeting with the agency, the lady with the earrings greeted us at reception. Jo whispered to me that it was indeed the nosey woman she met at the nail salon.

As we walked through their offices, the long halls glowed from unseen lights. When we turned a corner, we passed a Giacometti. The lady interrupted her explanation of the meeting to point at the heavy-footed stalagmite of bronze and said, 'Giacometti'.

'And if we can name a thing, we are its master,' I replied. Jo smiled and gave my hand a playful squeeze. The woman said how thrilling it was to have me present and what a privilege it was. Another corner, another plinth; this one held a mistake of flesh in a large jar. This Ġerhwek had the smallest hint of a tongue resting on a string of baby teeth peeking from behind the slanting lips of a stroke patient. It lay upon its own twirled nest of white nerves. We stopped once again, the lady's earrings plinking our halt.

She read the plaque aloud, '"Ceccaldi Ġerhwek, discovered by Cassandra." You'll meet Cassie today I hope. If the meeting goes well, the debut of the Martin Sutch Ġerhwek will be historic.' One more hallway and we were sat at the desk across from three women from the agency. Everyone was nice enough but they all looked alike and had the sort of names that car companies save for their family compacts. The expectation, the need, the unblinking grins from across the table made me sweat until I sat in a horrible soup of myself.

'Yakisugi?' I asked, examining the black and yellow waves in the grain of the desk between us. They nodded and the grins widened but no one said anything. Then one of them leapt up and declared, 'Cassandra!' as another woman joined us. The others stood. I did too but it seemed a faux pas. Cassandra chided the women for not offering coffee. A button was pushed and two women wearing tabards emerged from the wall. They set down trays. The rich orange of their wood, the rounded edges and the soft grey of the stoneware tea set were works of art, especially in contrast to the colours of the table. I kept my mouth shut. Jo matched every fake smile and trumped every compliment with one of her own. Still, there was something pleasurable about the fussiness of it all, the petit fours, the unrelenting beauty.

'Martin, may we?' Cassandra pointed a polished nail at my stomach. There was a thin grey line below her lip like the start of a Māori tattoo.

I stood and unbuttoned my shirt. They looked disappointed by the net curtain Jo had made to cover the porthole. I showed off the disc magnets she had sewn in it and demonstrated how it worked. There was some discussion about it. The phrase 'the brand' was used a lot. Jo tucked it away in her pocket, embarrassed. I explained that the thing seemed to quiet down, like a budgie, if you covered it. There were nights that its hum awoke me and pushed me to the window to witness the full moon obscured by thin clouds.

'That milky glow is more beautiful than a clearly seen moon,' I said. I stammered on about how the Gerhwek song vibrates through my body and into the floor until I feel water gurgling through the piping beneath, the mouse nest full of writhing pinkies anxious for their mother's milk, the neighbour-below's panicked dreams about a performance review he had at work. What I couldn't mention with Jo there were those other nights I lost hours weeping over Danny's

37

crib as he slept, his knees and arms pulled under him, knowing that at sixty-three, long after I am gone, he will die of bowel cancer, leaving his own wife and four children. Jo would only take in the overwhelming sadness of that last moment and not the beauty of the life entire. I was glad when the earrings lady let me know with her finely shaped brow that I needed to wrap up my discourse. So, I tapped the glass with my knuckles and said, 'showtime, my little mezzo soprano tumour.'

'Gerhwek, Martin,' she said, before the song took her.

I felt their thoughts as shapes. Cassandra's, which were daggers before, soon melded into the candy floss of the others.

After the song, in the silence, those still and perfectly groomed heads came back to the room, the threads of pink clearing like smoke.

Cassandra stood, the others stood, I didn't move.

'Bravo,' Cassandra said, not to me, but to Statement Earrings. I really should've remembered her name at this point. I'd heard Cassandra's name a million times and got the impression she was some sort of rival, but now, in this plush room, she seemed like the lady's biggest fan. 'You're going big, I hope,' Cassandra said. There were murmurs and suppressed squeals. While I sat and fidgeted, drinking too much coffee and eating the majority of the perfect cakes and biscuits, phrases such as 'all or nothing' and 'beyond billboards' pinged around the room. Jo continued chatting along with them, but I knew she was waiting for her moment. Cassandra was on her feet, pointing to the heavens, taking in the whole world with expansive gestures. Statement Earrings wiped an invisible tear from her eye.

The tabarded women emerged, carrying a scale model of the Festival Hall theatre. Immediately, Cassandra plucked the tiny queen from the royal box.

'If you recall, Her majesty is no longer available for the performance,' she said and handed it to the tabarded woman nearest with a sharp look. She pulled a tiny King Charles from her pocket. 'But I have no doubt that you'll secure the king's presence, for an event this momentous.'

As they discussed the colour scheme and staging, I suggested, 'if you moved these structures here it would create a tighter focal point around the centre of the stage, which would emphasise the solo nature of the performance.' They looked at me as if they had forgotten I was still in the room.

'Actually, there's something we haven't discussed,' Jo said, giving my knee a squeeze. She had her nails done for this moment, coloured black in a style called Stiletto. 'Compensation.' The women all looked aghast.

Earrings looked at Cassandra.

'This is *your* show,' Cassandra said in response, and there was a brief moment I felt bad for these women.

~

I've been returning to that fateful spot on the canal for several days now. I can't find the exact patch where the pigeon exploded; there's not so much as a stain on the broken tarmac, but the mood is the same: crap everywhere, above and below the oily water. While I stare at whatever

Martin was staring at when I followed him here, be it a rusty bike carcass or a mouldy sneaker, I try to imagine what he is doing now. Mostly, I fail.

When dusk fell that evening at the Festival Hall, everything shimmered, especially the future – Martin's, of course, though mainly mine. As my team encircled the champagne fountain in the VIP bar, and Cassandra made a toast, I held my breath. She reminded us of the great and good who would soon be pressed together in the stalls, speechless with wonder. Cassie had wangled us not just Charles but Camilla too; an ex-prime minister – not that one; the best of breakfast TV, Strictly and Bake Off. But in the front rows, thin-lipped smiles failing to disguise their envious rage, would be the upper echelons of Nightingale, Genie, and all of Auricle's longstanding rivals. Their eyes would flick now and then to the royal box, for they would know that above them perched representatives of the most prestigious international prizes known to our industry. How they would gulp. How our hearts would sing, as Martin Sutch's Ǵerhwek flooded the hall with its sublime gobbledegook, recalibrating an entire generation's scale of aesthetic wonder, lighting up all those piteous human brains with new meaning, soul-searing insight and above all, pleasure.

As the VIP bar began to swim with expensive perfumes, silk scarves and rarefied accents, I watched Martin, still incognito, ushering his wife and child to the plate glass windows overlooking the glittering Thames. How different from that stagnant strip of canal, with its unhygienic benches and decomposing dog turds. Here was elevation, here was electricity; the great institutes of British art and politics crowded along the water's edge, gazing up in search of the Sutch Gerhwek.

His wife spread her manicured talons against the glass, nails varnished obsidian. Martin scooped up a handful of vol-au-vents from a passing waiter's silver platter and dropped them into his jacket pocket. As I smiled indulgently, Cassandra caught my eye.

'I can't wait,' she hissed. She had already presented me with my own gold propeller-pencil, an exact replica of the one she now twirled between her fingers in agitated expectation.

I relate this happy moment, lullabied by the hum of celebrity chatter, bathed in the famous light of the South Bank's illuminations, because what followed is harder for me to describe. The whole period, from the moment Cassie conceded and gave me her unstinting support, to the last pitter-patter of the applause that welcomed Martin to the stage, had been a kind of dream, turned pastel and fuzzy by the glaze of wish-fulfilment. I had floated from Martin's darling net curtain to the eye-watering budget for his launch, as if in the movie version of my life. The camera had zoomed in on luxury patisseries, benevolent nods from superiors and a certain pair of eloquent intestinal lips, and in the distance had been a glow, the raspberry-ripple sunrise of my own ascent.

Sunrises are actually quite disappointing compared with sunsets. I know: I've tried them out from Rhodes to Chichen Itza. What occurred in the Festival Hall had all the drama, all the pathos, all the heart-breaking scale of a sunset, but none of the beauty.

Martin, pockets still bulging with overpriced and under-sized pastry, took up his place centre stage. The spotlight picked out the sweat on his forehead and the creases in his suit. But, he did his duty and unscrewed the port. He even managed a moment of dramatic pause, a suggestion from the dramaturge we hired at great expense. I grabbed Pandora's hand and closed my eyes.

~

All their love bombing and big promises, never mind what-ever office politics Cassandra and Earrings were playing at, had all worked to Jo's strategy. She was going to get as much as we could up front. There would be no stringing this out. She had played the quiet country mouse and they weren't quite prepared for a girl who grew up playing beneath her grandparent's market stall.

That night, although I was alone behind the curtain wish-ing she and Danny were there, our bond tethered us together. I fingered the greasy vol-au-vents I couldn't eat, knuckling crumbs into my pocket seams. Then the stage manager nodded, and I stepped out and onto my mark. The light leak beneath the curtain ebbed and the murmur of the audience stilled. This was it. Do this and our family will be okay.

The curtain rose. Mercifully, most of the hall was lost in darkness but the hard and forceful pressure of their attention was a stone on my chest. The light of the stage reached Jo and Danny though. I focused on them. Jo looked great. I had urged her to splurge. Her nails *and* hair done to perfection. Little man was there in her lap. He watched the vibrations between us dance. She had dressed him in a suit to match my own, including a blue bowtie. My suit had been tailored to reveal the port with a single motion. Before I did, I paused to look at Jo. I had glued a small blue bowtie to the port. She smiled and shook her head. She loves it when I'm cheeky. I opened the port with a flourish and a wink to her and the rest of the night disappeared.

~

Silence from the stalls. Not rapt silence, not pin-drop silence. The silence of complete, cruel indifference.

From the wings, I looked to our highest-value tastemakers. The queen consort had her head in her hands. The Breakfast TV host was tapping something urgently into a mobile phone. I searched the atmosphere for the static of sensory rapture, and picked up only bored fury.

As if underwater, as if drowning, I forced my gaze back towards Martin. There he stood, gazing with unalloyed love at his family in the sixth row, stretching out the lapels of his new jacket to amplify the wail from his belly, oblivious to the disdain that flooded from the audience in waves so strong they should have knocked him over.

Afterwards, I saw Martin and his wife kissing like teen-agers, tumbling into the folds of the fire curtain, happy as a pair of kittens. But I was numb by then, from the polite applause and the stampede from the seats towards the nearest exit. Streams of people desperate to get into a pub and howl with laughter at the folly, the joke, presented to them as a jewel.

I might have coped with general incomprehension. It can take decades for genius to be appreciated. I might have sat back, dug in, and waited for the Nobel prize that would follow a thousand increasingly astounded think-pieces, writers grappling with their own inability to parse the Sutch Ġerhwek at first hearing. But as Martin strode off the stage and into his wife's unsophisticated embrace, it was Cassandra who stood next to me and pinched my elbow.

'Shame,' she said. I heard the crunch of graphite. When she grinned, her teeth shone battleship grey. 'You know, it's all in the archives at Auricle.' She was digging in her Birkin, dragging out something thin and claggy that stuck to her fingers. 'The first embedded Ġerhwek. Nearly finished me, at the time.'

Her laugh landed as leaden spittle on my cheek as she slapped the dead Ġerhwek into my own palm.

'It's not embedded,' I said, batting away the truth.

'Oh, it was. But you know, the humiliation, the abject failure. We'd been so sure. Just like you. Made total fools of ourselves.' She wiped her mouth.

How I wish I'd had the gumption to snatch that golden pencil and jab it up under her ribs. Instead, I sloped away, with that rotten oyster of her revenge quivering in my hand.

I had planned to throw it into the canal, but there's nothing left of it now except a smear of gunge on a Festival Hall napkin. I searched in the putrid green water, day after day, seeking Martin's artistic vision, sifting for the way of seeing that made him Ǵerhwek-worthy. But all I saw was rotting junk. What was it that had shone from his eyes, even as his audience wilted? A kind of aliveness, a oneness with his Ǵerhwek's wail that made him, somehow, happier. That made his wife and son gaze back at him with admiring adoration. I wanted it, more than I wanted my job at Auricle back.

Today, staring down into the canal, I made out a drowned mobility scooter ridden through the swirling murk by a mossy traffic cone. I don't know what it was that tipped me over the edge. Pity, maybe, or revulsion. The sheer demented ugliness of it all. But I felt the purest, cleanest sadness I had ever felt. The shock of it was almost pleasurable. I let the feeling well up around me, obliterating all else.

At that very moment, I heard a wet sort of pop. I watched a dandelion sprout and grow as if in a time-lapse film. It threw its leaves out from the crack in the pavement, shot its stem upward; a bud burst into a firework of yellow petals, retracted, burst forth again into the fuzz of its clock before the seeds dispersed and the plant shrivelled and died away.

Hope welled in within me. This was an Event.

I scanned left and right, desperate not to find a Chosen One standing there. There was nobody but me. So I waited in ecstasy for a searing pain in my belly to prove that I, too, was: Lucky, Original, Validated and Exceptional.

~

I hear him on the phone. The way he refers to me as 'my wife' like he can't believe his luck. He's a good man. The momentary celebrity was enough for the university to come back, hat in hand, with apologies and a professorship. I'm used to the little window they cut into him. At first the circle of brass, like a dinner plate held against his skin, still red and irritated by the surgery, broke my heart. It's not supposed to be there, is all I thought. Now, I see it as a gift to us from those women. Never 'Ǵerhwek'. That was their name.

Danny always wants to be near his dad. They babble to each other, our little boy and Martin's gift. He runs his diecast cars across the porthole glass, back and forth until inevitably he nestles against his father's unique belly. Martin's huge hands blanket Danny's shoulders and he reads him a book until our son falls asleep.

# The Girl Chewing Gum

## Adrian Duncan & Jo Lloyd

*A series of fictions inspired by a woman who appears for a few moments in the 1976 film* The Girl Chewing Gum, *by the artist John Smith.*

### Chess

The girl chewing gum walks past Steele's on the corner.

Half an hour before, during lunch hour, she'd gone to her shared house on Downham Road to pick up her savings book. From there, she'd walked north on Mortimer Road and, where it met a narrow terrace, had called into a corner shop for a packet of chewing gum and a small sausage roll. Then she made her way, through a fragrant breeze, into De Beauvoir Gardens, where, at her usual bench, sat two men engaged in a game of chess, one cradling a bottle of whiskey wrapped in paper. She took a seat at the next bench over, under the shade of an expansive beech tree.

She ate her sausage roll, gazing up at the white light flickering through the leaves. One of the men to her right, the one with the whiskey bottle, stood, his arms raised in what she took, as she finished her sausage roll, to be delight. The other man, still seated at the chessboard, shook his head. His playing partner danced in a small circle, took a sip from his bottle and sat back down.

Some birds fluttered off.

She rose and made her way towards the northern corner of the garden, which was beginning to fill with people surging from the surrounding offices and businesses to take lunch and enjoy some fresh air.

This young woman walked on in her old platform shoes, still pinching at the heels, up Mortimer Road to where it met Englefield Road, where she waited to allow traffic to pass, before breaking into a run across the carriageway. Passing a newsagents, she took in a crowd gathering outside the Odeon in the distance. Then pausing, she tried to unpick a piece of sausage roll from between her two rear-most left molars, wondering, as her third finger touched the patch of bare gum beyond these two teeth, if a wisdom tooth might yet appear. A fire alarm in the distance began to trill. The piece of sausage roll would not come free so she tongued it a while instead, standing there on the busy pavement of a lunchtime Stamford Road. Then she took a chewing-gum stick from its packet and bent it into her mouth.

She began to chew and walk and chew, the juices gathering in her mouth, until she crossed Tottenham Road, where she lingered for a boy on a bicycle to spin by. As she passed Steele's, she looked to her right and saw, across the road, a young man with a camera on a tripod, in the act of tilting his camera down from the sky to the street. She looked a moment longer as the cameraman captured her walking past Steele's, a company in the business of fabricating mirrors, shelves and table tops.

## Prince Charles

On Jackie's first day at school, after crying, singing, listening to a story, then crying some more, they played with plasticine. Little girls with ribbons in their hair rolled out snake after snake. Jackie made horses and dogs. Oh! the other children said, looking at her stumpy creations like they'd been carved in Michelangelo's workshop. After that, all the way through school, art was her thing.

In careers, they asked if she'd thought about art college. But her parents wanted her to do something practical. You can always do a bit of painting in your spare time, said her mother. Like Prince Charles.

Jackie thought about Prince Charles sometimes, later, as she was trudging through one practical office job after another. Alphabetising five years of booking slips or pasting corrections into stacks of misspelt handouts. She wondered if Prince Charles ever questioned his choices.

The offices were all the same. The men were upstairs and 'the girls' were downstairs, arranged in rows like in a classroom. They had to ask permission to have a drink of water or go to the toilet.

At one place, a manager asked her to stay late to finish a report. He came down to collect it. Thank you, he said,

51

standing too close. You don't have to thank me, she said. Still, thank you, he said. You don't have to thank me, she repeated. But I want to thank you, he said. I'm not doing it as a fucking favour, I get paid, she said, picking up her coat. She didn't wait to listen to his reply.

~

## French cigarette

The girl chewing gum walks past Steele's on the corner. Some moments before, she'd spied a young man across the road, hunched behind a camera and tripod, tilting the camera from the clock above Steele's down to the shining street.

This cameraman has curly dark hair and is dressed in black. If she were to guess, she would say that he is not from the BBC; if she were to guess, she would say that he is an art student, soon to look up from his camera, frown, place a cap over the camera's lens, and then smoke, pensively – surely – a French cigarette.

A car drives past.

Behind the distant cameraman, two men appear, one long, one small, both exiting a building whose use is hard to discern – a small claims court? An insurer's?

Jackie looks back at the cameraman, now panning his camera to the left, and she can see, on the side of his mouth, the beginnings of a smile. She pushes her hair over her shoulder: who said it was okay for that creep to point that thing at me? As she makes off down Stamford Road, she imagines her face some day projected large in an otherwise darkened hall.

Across the road, unnoticed yet by Jackie, is Maurice Kelly Junior. He's been away from London and only returned to the neighbourhood recently. He is now a member of a group of casuals who travel every second weekend to football games around the country, to sway and sing in decrepit stadia and then begin brawls of at-first-unknowable dimensions, brawls that, Maurice hopes in those moments before it truly 'kicks off', will grow to inconceivable degrees of spite and destruction. Last month, at a game in Manchester, he and fifteen others stormed a flank of Victoria Station, leaving a trail of havoc in their wake. They were clubbed by a column of policemen at the top of the southern entrance, and then ushered between two rows of mounted police to Piccadilly where they were eased onto a train heading south. It was here, while they passed bottles of vodka and tins of beer from one to the other, that Maurice decided, for the first time in almost a year, to visit home.

## Bugs and bits of plants

Jackie had always avoided Maurice at school, him and his mates, with their smart mouths. But then one day he came up to her in the corner shop and started chatting like they were best friends.

Come on, he said. Let's go.

He was 17 then, had already left school, and she was 16. He never asked if she liked him and for months she didn't ask herself. There was something dark in him and she wanted to see what it was.

53

Sometimes she'd borrow money from her Nan, or Maurice'd get a few quid for helping his dad on the allotment, and then they might go to the Odeon, sit at the back wrapped round each other (whole films she'd missed, couldn't tell you who got happy-ever-after and who got sacrifice and mourning) or to The Lion or The Cups, find a dim corner where no one would question their age, and she'd have lager top or cider-and-black and Maurice would work his way through pints like he was in training. But more often they had 27p between them, plus half a pack of Embassy Reds Maurice had begged from his dad, and they'd go to the graveyard or the top of the multi-storey, their private realms of dirt and crisp packets and broken bottles and ivy. Bugs and bits of plant falling off her when she got home.

~

## Muse

The girl chewing gum walks past Steele's on the corner. As she gazes down the camera lens for some moments, it strikes the cameraman, looking back at her through these concave slivers of glass, that she, a woman he has not seen before, will certainly become the muse for this film. The nature, duration and tone of the film, he realises, though, is still far from his grasp. He whispers to himself as she turns away and exits the right of the frame: *The world and all of its contents are but a fleeting Cartesian theatre over and across of which appear multitudes and delights*. Then, silently tutting, he dismisses this overwrought line and looks up at the street beyond his whirring camera. A bus then a lorry pass, both throatily pluming exhaust into the air, obscuring this gum-chewing girl as she disappears around a corner.

She turns right at the next junction, then up past the Odeon, outside which snakes a queue, awaiting the afternoon matinee of *Logan's Run*.


**Fancy piece**

The Odeon struggled for some years, finally shutting down in 1979.

They're closing the Odeon, Jackie said to her mother, in lieu of more difficult conversations.

I remember it opening, said her mother.

Really? said Jackie, struck by the revelation that the cinema had had a beginning. When was that?

Nan took me to the ribbon cutting. Who did it? One of those starlets with that blonde hair. A fancy piece, Nan would have said. You know how she was.

Sylvia meant Jackie's Nan, her own mother, dead then, but not forgiven for the things she'd put Sylvia through: hand-me-downs, rationing, the foreign name on her birth certificate and its later anglicising, cabbage soup, sheets turned sides-to-middle, the discouragement, perhaps, of an intellectual young man who might otherwise have provided the epic passion of Sylvia's life, forever casting a what-if shade over her eventual marriage to solid Frank, who refused to take his wife to the cinema, saying, why would I want to watch a made-up story?

55

Sylvia liked to have her last cigarette of the day outside in the darkness, no matter what the weather or time of the year. She smoked with concentration and efficiency, as if getting through that filter tip was a task she'd been asked to accomplish before she could lay down her head. She did not look up at whatever grand plots were being projected across the heavens nor even around to bins, shrubs, a late cat negotiating a boundary, but straight ahead, to where the air hung opaque under the street lamps and a few cars lolled at an angle, and beyond that to windows, and then smaller windows, and finally just a blur giving off light.

~

### Shoes

The girl chewing gum walks past Steele's on the corner. Some moments before, the cameraman across the street, hearing a commotion in the queue outside the Odeon at the end of the road, looked up and lost his train of thought. She lost hers too, taking in his young oval face and his deep dark eyes frowning down the street. He looked over and she peered instead at her feet, noticing a rip across the toes of her shoes, a gift of some years back from her Nan. She looked up once more, but he was back to tending his camera.

## Kingsland Road

Jackie's Nan had come up against some of the great events of the century in her youth and it had left her with a dim view of human nature. People were a kind of freight, Nan thought, some more literally so than others, carried about the world haphazardly until they were unloaded on a random quayside, there to spend the rest of their days staring at the sky in puzzlement.

When Jackie was small, Nan took care of her while Sylvia was at work. One December, after Sylvia left, Nan went round taking down all the tinsel and homemade paper chains that Sylvia had put up the day before. Finally she took the Christmas tree and dragged it out onto the pavement, baubles and all.

That afternoon she took Jackie out shopping with her. Potatoes, cornflour, and a Pyrex bowl were on her list. The short day had ended and the air was spacious and cold. When they reached the high street it was to find it strung with stars and angels and ropes of glittering lights. Nan held Jackie's hand and walked too fast for Jackie to comfortably take in the transfiguration, grumbling unseasonably.

We pay for this road, Nan said. And then she started talking quickly, her accent growing dense and tangled. Something about Romans and Celts and Africans and yes, Jews.

When Jackie was older she understood that her Nan was talking about the Roman road that ran beneath Kingsland Road, and their distant ancestors who had marched along it, footsore and cold and dreaming of olive groves and

57

the bright globes of pomegranates. Whether this was true was not the point for Nan. Her view of history was more argumentative than reflective.

Always remember we were here before the English, Nan said. Meaning *we* in the wider sense, Nan herself having been born in Lithuania.

When she was older still, Jackie would stop putting up Christmas decorations. She would take Hebrew lessons and study the Torah. She and Rosa would visit Lithuania. Jackie wished then that she'd asked her Nan more questions. She had inherited only disarticulated fragments, bones and wiring scattered about an attic.

Those blackshirt cunts weren't even here when this road was built, said Nan. Don't let them tell you different.

Nan's English was not perfect and it is possible she thought cunts meant something else.

That evening, when Frank got home, he moved the Christmas tree back inside and nobody discussed its temporary absence or why it now had the forlorn and startled appearance of a rescue dog.

~

## Bridge

The girl chewing gum walks past Steele's on the corner. Inside, against the window leans a middle-aged woman wearing a baggy and patterned jumper. Some moments after Jackie passes, the woman turns to look out at the street, her broad face unimpressed. This woman had been enquiring once more after Maurice Kelly Senior, Steele's assistant-head glazier, who'd not been into work for the last week. Many in the place were concerned, not least of all her – Maurice Senior was her bridge partner.

This woman in the patterned jumper will call over to Maurice's house later that night and find no one there. She'll push the side door open and see the insides ransacked and she'll think, in the cool glinting dark, of what he said to her, on the way home from their last evening of bridge, about his only son.


## Harmless

When Jackie broke up with Maurice it took a while to stick. He'd forget and call her and she'd forget and answer. The last time was just before Maurice went away. She was at her mother's. He probably didn't even know she'd moved out. OK, she said into the phone, turning as if that could stop Sylvia hearing. Yup. OK.

You still go running when that one calls? said Sylvia. Stories I hear about him, you wouldn't believe.

He's harmless, Jackie said.

That's what they said about Hitler.

Did they though? Jackie said. Did they really say that about Hitler?

Sylvia sniffed to show how far above authentication her discourse sailed. I thought you had more sense, she said.

Jackie thought so too but she didn't stop to answer, just picked up her bag and headed out.

Her route took her past Steele's, where Maurice's dad worked. She'd never asked what Mr Kelly did there but she'd always imagined him alone in a vast room, polishing fabricated surfaces to a hushed glassy sheen. Perhaps he liked his job, perhaps he hummed as he worked. Perhaps he'd like Maurice to follow him into the fabrication trade.

Even Mr Kelly had warned her off Maurice. She stopped and stared at the pavement as if it might impart some ancient wisdom.

~

## Maurice

The girl chewing gum walks past Steele's on the corner. She makes off down the street once more, when she hears, from across the way, a familiar voice. Jackie! it calls, Jackie!

Her stomach crumples.

Jackie!

She utters a low ugh.

Jackie!

A car horn blows, and as she turns to cross the thoroughfare, she calls – now grimacing into a smile: Maurice. You're back.

She crosses the road, as the two men who were exiting the large building opposite moments ago stop alongside the cameraman to see what it is he is capturing and enquire as to the model of the camera and how much it might cost.

The cameraman looks up and shrugs.

Where are you off to, Jackie? says Maurice, grinning, as he looks her up and down.

She takes in a newly-carved scar across his neck.

Jackie, where...

Work, she says. I'm off to work.

They shift their weight and, as the wind switches, the sun comes back out, making Maurice squint and raise a hand to his eyes.

What time do you finish? he asks.

Five or so, she replies.

Still at your mum's?

Sometimes, says Jackie, sometimes not...

I'm around for a while.

Oh... that's nice.

Yeah, I'll be around for a while, Jackie.

Right. Well good to see you again, Maurice. Good to see you are back in town. I'd better go.

Maurice stays where he is, waiting for Jackie to turn.

She sees behind him the cameraman collapsing his tripod and putting it over his shoulder. The cameraman looks at her a moment, then he turns and makes off towards a bus stop at the end of the street.

Jackie walks away and Maurice peers after her for some time. Then he crosses the street towards Steele's, enters and asks the people gathered there if his father, Maurice Kelly Senior, is available to speak to for a moment. They shake their heads, saying they've not seen him for almost a week. He asks once more, holding on to the timber-panelled reception desk, strewn with paper. He stays until he is sure he has made impression enough that this is the first he's heard of his father's disappearance.

On the pavement outside, the cameraman looks over his shoulder once more, as he lifts his unlit cigarette to his lips. Then he sprints after a bus pulling into a bus stop almost thirty yards away. The cameraman gallops, his dark curls bobbing in the breeze. He slaps the side of the bus and jumps on, moments before the bus accelerates down the street, then lurches right.

Some miles along the road, the cameraman realises that the can of film he'd unloaded from his camera has been forgotten at the side of the street opposite Steele's.


## A mess of red

In 1982, the land where the Odeon stood was sold for redevelopment. When they started pulling the cinema down, it seemed to endure their attentions for some time unaffected and then, overnight almost, the exterior walls and roof were gone. For three days the tiered seats hung in the air, exposed to unscreened reality: the sun falling into a mess of red, the stars wheeling round East London, the sky dropping sparrows and starlings and rain and soot and pollen and small invertebrates. The noise of engines was thunderous, it made the seats tremble. Dustbin lids clattered. Glass smashed. Alarms rang and stopped and rang. A faulty streetlight buzzed all night. A fox floated past, soundless, its feet not touching the ground. In the darkest, smallest hours a blackbird sang, impossibly huge, and late walkers and early wakers mistook it for something else.

Every day, Jackie went past the construction site, thinking sometimes of films she had seen there and the people she'd been with, of the people she'd since lost, and the nature of loss and time, but more often of work and love and money and what she would have for her tea.

~

## Rain

The girl chewing gum walks past Steele's on the corner. The cameraman is across the road setting up his camera to try to replicate the framing from his last day of shooting. He's since got a loan from some friends and bought new rolls of stock, one of which he'll load onto the camera in less than an hour, just as it begins to thunder with rain. Then he'll pack up once more, on the cusp of forgoing this project, but will nonetheless return a few days hence and record the happenings once more.

## Implacable and serene

In the summer of 1984, not long after they met, Jackie went with Rosa to one of the GLC's free festivals on the South Bank. The Smiths were playing, Billy Bragg, Black Uhuru. Every single person there was in agreement about everything: reclaiming the night and freeing Nelson Mandela and ending Cruise missiles. It was like visiting the future, where everyone would know what was good and how to achieve it, and the music would be glorious.

Jackie and Rosa sat on the ground beneath the benevolent sun. When Rosa's friends Nasreen and Cerys arrived,

Rosa sprang up to greet them. Jackie, new and shy, watched for a while, and then took photos of them, shooting into the sun. She'd only had the camera a couple of weeks and didn't know what she was doing, but when she got the prints back from Boots she was pleased. The light effect left nothing visible of their ordinary selves, not their thoughts or worries, not the fine lines time had left on their faces. They glowed, implacable and serene, like goddesses. I can do this, Jackie thought. This is what I want to do.

On the way back to the Tube, she and Rosa got into a stupid argument about the Smiths and Black Uhuru. Rosa had been making a subtle political point that Jackie had not fully understood and arguing against it did not make it clearer.

Later, as they hurtled beneath London, Rosa reached for Jackie's hand. Sorry, she said, although it was Jackie who should have been saying sorry. Their fingers touched and they glowed like goddesses. Their light filled the carriage and flared on the dark walls outside.

~

## Sobbing

The girl chewing gum walks past Steele's on the corner.

Half an hour before, she'd left Downham Road. She'd gone north onto Mortimer Road and, where it met a narrow terrace, called into a corner shop for a packet of chewing gum and a small sausage roll.

She walked up Englefield and on to Stamford Road, then, deciding to leave her sausage roll until evening, she wrapped it in a serviette, and instead bent a stick of chewing gum into her mouth.

As she passes Steele's on the corner, she looks to her right and sees once more that cameraman, now dressed in a long duffle coat. A line of smoke emerges from behind his glinting camera as he tilts the lens down from the clock above Steele's to the quiet street below.

This time he hasn't noticed the girl chewing gum passing on the street beyond because he's focused on the back of the woman in the window of Steele's. She has her head in her hands. Her shoulders, under her patterned jumper, through the dusty murk of the windows, seem to be shaking. It looks as if this woman is sobbing.

A police car pulls out of the yard to the rear of Steele's, turns right, then passes the Odeon, where a crowd gathers, waiting to procure tickets for the last matinee showing of *Logan's Run*.

The girl chewing gum, this Jackie, passes. She looks up for a moment, as the fluorescent lamps inside the Odeon flicker to life.

# Morphic Resonance

## Roelof Bakker & David Rose

### CLOUD

A smell enters the shop, a scent, sudden, brought in on the breeze,
the draught through the door, different from the smell inside,
fruit, lettuce, cucumber, it's          can't place it, from far back,
can't connect     the cloud, can't connect to the      I have to
there was a blue dress, or     eyes? blue eyes? where? I have to
focus, connect it all
pushed, I'm being pushed, jostled, people are      the queue,
holding up the queue, I must move, move out of their     into the
fresh air, but someone's pulling at me, shouting      pay, I have to
pay   of course, I always pay, I've always paid, never not paid,
never walked out without
easy now, tap my card, easy now, now fumbling   coins in odd
pockets        only carrots and potatoes, not worth lifting, why
would I, why would they think
breathe deep, calm           stronger now, the scent     plants,
a rack outside the shop, bedding plants, petunias, geraniums,

salvias  not    here,  it's  from  this,  the  smell  is  coming  from
this   below   the   rack,   larger   pots,   shrubs,   hydrangeas     one
of    this one, small blue flowers, intense      Lobelia the label    not
the  bedding  type,  shrubby,  twiggy,  perennial  it  says   pick it up
I  can  smell  foliage  sunbruised  like  sage     think  carefully,
where   would       park?  only   bedding   type   there,   mixed,
interplanted    salvias
garden?    large  garden?  lawn,  a  lake,  there  was  a  lake,  far
off    heat,  hot  day,  hoses,  the  spiralling  kind,  jetting  up,  making
rainbows      bench, I was   *we were* on a bench    wood warm, rough
in  places,  splintered     we sat close  blue eyes, lobelia-blue    yes,
dress, matched    we kissed     who was   *is*  is she still     might
be  dead,  if  so,  down  to  me,  my  responsibility,  to  remember,
preserve     otherwise  for  her    Second  Death          misery
endures, is endurable but happiness evaporates, in time          those
moments  burden  of    bright  shafts  of  sunlight  breaking
the     years, must be      all those years     waste sad years  live
day to day    withdrawn, retracted, the tortoise sleeps
better so? safer so?

## EYE

I see a lone tortoise in the water, swimming towards the edge of the lake, approaching me and two strangers. Once near shore, the reptile's head pops up above the water and looks at us as if about to say something. Face to face with the dapper beast, a woman exclaims with firm earnestness: 'beautiful!' This moment is a video record from another decade, a slice of life in ten slithery seconds to be played and replayed, to live and live again. No regrets.

I see in the hallway mirror a vertically-flipped impression of a man quite different in appearance from the reflection a year ago, two years ago, five years, ten, twenty, thirty years ago. If I go back many more years, no image will show. Forward in time, at some irreversible point, the mirror will be empty, my image erased forever. Happily today the mirror is my accomplice, confirms yet again I exist.

I see a bearded, chunky lad leaving the branch of a McDonalds located strategically beside a busy roundabout. On the back of his grey hoody, two words, stitched in all caps, state: 'GET LAID'. Does he?

I see from the train window a wood of tall birch trees, foliage merging like a Monet painting as the carriage rushes by. I see a small area demarcated by bright-coloured tape fixed around the trunks of trees, creating a circle, a round exclusion zone. Three wreaths of red flowers – roses? – lie at the base of one old tree in the centre of the zone. An accident, murder, suicide?

I see you.

# FLOWER

face    time to face        all those years    evaporated a long
parched    aestivation    face up to the    mirror    so much forgotten
disappeared    past recall    like my reflection    parts missing
as with a migraine    features unrecognised a slow what's
the word *excoriation* I behold my face as in a glass and
straightaway forget the man I face    have to
face up to responsibility    *for now we see through a glass darkly, but
then, face to* face the burden, redeem the memories own up    for
I have been happy, I'm convinced    must call    chemist, pick
up my    prescription, all the packets, pills, get home fill the little
compartments, marked    *give us this day* I                feel
sometimes like Timothy Leary    later, though, must sit for a while,
order    clear my brain    there's a bench here

        metal though, hot to the touch but
rainbows I remember    what else    roses, laid out symmetrically,
formal beds, standards behind, floribunda in front    where was
this?    she said quick, while no one's    I picked one, tight
bud, presented it to her    folded it into tissue popped into
her handbag    hands, held hands as we followed the path,
followed the signs to    where?


    rockery,    gravel    surround    then    stone
chippings    *scree*    delicate alpines, gentians yes, saxifrage
tight between rocks, dwarf pines, their resinous scent mixing
chiming with hers as I held her hand    we stepped carefully

70

on flat rocks like flagstones until       huge rock, shade, come in under    not red though, grey    leant against as we sat, I said, a friendly monolith    *lithium* where it's from?
shady, but the rock was warm    soaks up the warmth, stores against the winter    maybe our task too, absorb, retain the memories against that eternity of   cold    we hopped stone by stone back to the grass, followed the wall    where *was* this?

## ←TO THE LION GATE

before the exit, a lake dazzling in the light but not water, white    raked gravel    then bamboo, clipped pines, a gate, ornamental gate, Japanese? yes we kissed, we kissed beneath the gate a red pagoda above the trees    *Kew* it was in Kew yes sky still unclouded but turning to cobalt high above    clearer, becoming clearer now    those paper flowers that unfold in water

how   much   more   to excavate    brush  away  the  sand, uncover a    settlement, a world    still a patient    a slow retrieving    retrieval of my    Self

# STONE

I see a glass of wine one-quarter full. Wish I hadn't hit that bottle of red. Restless, awkward sleep in the armchair. Nightmares. Dreams.

I swim towards the bottom of the ocean looking for a door I've shut behind me *(for I have been happy, I'm convinced)*, hoping to unlock it *(yes we kissed)*. When I find it, I turn the key *(Kew it was Kew yes sky still unclouded)*.

As I rise, I make a firm decision to go back to southwest London to walk across the rose gardens, scale the pagoda, maybe visit the Palm House. Put myself in a place of past time, hoping for recollections, however flimsy or cloudy.

A hangover my company, I travel on the Underground, not entirely sure I've taken my medication.

I see the word ahead of me, printed on a poster above a carriage window: 'starling'. Anything about birds grabs my attention, so I read on, expecting a Poem on the Underground.

It actually reads 'staring'. A poster warning about staring. Here we sit face to face – how can we but not stare? 'May lead to prosecution.' Human curiosity. Boredom. Sexual desire. Many reasons to stare. 'Sexual offence.'

I am thrilled to be going back to the gardens tracing paths she and I once walked on, past scented roses, colours bright and alive. I imagine our eyes meeting. Did we kiss there?

No, not the rose garden. It happened most definitely beneath the gate that led to the pagoda. When she spotted it, she exclaimed, 'Oh look! A kissing gate!'

A robotic voice shouts in my ears. Interrupts my visual flow. I was happy lingering, continuing together towards the pagoda. The voice commands, 'change here for the Circle and District Lines'.

The train pulls into Victoria station. That was quick. I grab my bag and stand up, perhaps a little too fast, feeling unexpectedly dizzy and disorientated. Unstable. As I step out, I trip over.

Stone.

feeling a little dizzier today the pills the side effects the therapist did warn me but it's fine they're beginning to take effect I think   I detect     I feel I'm gathering my wits or wit I feel an occasional lift an upswing moments even minutes of a hesitant euphoria a general falling away of the nagging fears things falling into place into normality.

Leary. The therapist asked me if I remembered Timothy Leary. Uncanny. I'd been thinking of him only recently I began to worry she was reading my mind

tapping my memory **entanglement** that's absurd of course she's trying to help I know that that's her job after all I see what she's trying to do see her strategy.

She said halfway into the session do you remember Timothy Leary? I said of course I do I'm a child of the Sixties – though remind me (feeling my power of repartee returning). She summed up his lifelong experiments in the pharmaceutical field then got to the crux the nub of how he ended up with Alzheimer's yet, remaining positive, said this was what he'd been looking for all his life it made entering his living room a daily adventure. I expected her to talk about *being in the moment*. Instead she asked if I felt a reluctance to make new memories, did I feel I had a 'Demon of Resistance' sitting on my shoulder.

She told me though to beware of false memories that they can be deceptive treacherous. I've been puzzling over the pagoda. A vague memory of climbing the stairs looking out over the trees across the Thames towards the City then walking round to look the other way to

Windsor Castle the leaves beginning to russet so early autumn dusk and hearing the polyphony of starlings **Twittering Machine** in full throstle as they swirled and settled but coming from far below me I was high above their roost the cacophony drifting up.

Yet there's another memory glint of the pagoda doors locked with Danger notices pinned to them. Is one false one true or both false or both true

need to know. Need to check.


Next day to the library. The only book they have on Kew is an old guidebook from 1967 with a nice period photo of the pagoda of my memory but I am in luck the librarian finds online an official website and gives me a printout.

According to the website the pagoda was accessible until the late 1980s when it was closed to the public due to its dilapidation. It's now open again after being fully restored. So my visits to Kew in the seventies eighties would have allowed for that climb and the murmuration equally the padlocked doors approaching the millennium were real.


But then there's the dragons. Do I remember the dragons? The website describes the original pagoda having gilded dragons on every floor, which rotted over the years and only restored recently, and in plastic not wood. Here then is a what's the word **ontological** conundrum. Which is the authentic pagoda? The one with dragons intact which lasted for only twenty two years, or the pagoda that then existed through two hundred years of natural decay, or the presently restored pagoda – which is the pagoda of my memory? These are not for me abstract puzzles and I've been trying to tease out the implications all night until my brain wearied. But I'm cheered now by the encouragement I get from this regarding the    similar restoration of my memory my own need or imperative to sharpen the details the dragons of my own pagoda and the realisation that the reconstituted memory is the only one now existing and for as long as I can retain it.

But there lies the terror.

# BODY

Falling out of the train, I experience the strangling rush of terror, my body collapsing onto the platform. A young woman, her neck blushing, enquires if I'm hurt. Do I have a headache? Do I feel nauseous? Any bones broken, ligaments torn? My replies satisfy her and she reaches out her hand to pull me up. A surprisingly firm grip. Blood rushes to my cheeks. Embarrassed, I recompose myself. I walk to the opposite platform. No Kew today.

No, I didn't tell my therapist about that mishap. I'm not sure it is the kind of new memory she wants me to collect. Such a folly anyhow to travel all that way, hoping that being near that old tower would help evoke pictures of her, make me rehear words once spoken, see her smile again.

The photograph on the cover of the 1967 Kew Gardens guide shows a small group of schoolgirls walking along the Broad Walk on a sunny day in polite knee-length dresses, an image far removed from the wild catwalk of Carnaby Street that summer. I didn't hang out much in Soho back then, but recalling Timothy Leary, I remember a bunch of us taking LSD at Finsbury Park, a Jimi Hendrix gig. Soon cascading flowers were all around me, covered me and everyone else. The voice of an angel sang, 'don't know if I'm coming up or down'. Then a fire started on stage, Hendrix going up in flames, thick clouds of smoke. It was absolute mayhem everyone towards the exit. Then a bucket of

77

water thrown over me and I'm standing in this pond, the water cool and calming, the moon bright and piercing. What did my therapist say again? Be Happy In The Moment. I was. She was. We kissed. We were euphoric. We were Extremely Happy In That Particular Moment.

As this happened over fifty years ago and we were high at the time, how real is it? The therapist warned me about unreliable memories. Perhaps my recollections are semi-fictional, the mind tweaking a manuscript, adding and cutting.

I see everything and nothing at all. I was informed it may take a few days, in some cases even weeks before the special effects wear off.

I've been staying off the wine since my incident, yet I continue to experience visual interruptions, like seeing *her,* ghost-like in my home, slouched in the armchair, her lips moving though no sound is made.

We met at Kew a week after the gig. A proper date. She had this thing about dragons. Apparently the pagoda had dragons with long eerie tongues. Could we go there first? But the beasts had long gone. I could see her disappointment. I put my arm around her to comfort her. Some workers were doing repairs. They let us sneak in. We went straight up to the top. An adventure! She smiled again. Blue eyes beaming. The views! Not sure now if it was autumn. We kissed for what seemed like hours, scattered leaves the last thing on our minds. Afterwards, we held hands, strolling down an avenue of cedars and found a bench under a tree. She'd made sandwiches. I'd brought a flask.

She said she liked the taste of my coffee, but we didn't say much more. The conversation was unexpectedly awkward, the silences even more so. We kissed again but it felt mechanical, as if she didn't want to anymore. I pulled away, feeling rejected. Did I misread her?

Then she said she had to go to the loo. We didn't say much when we walked up and she avoided all eye contact. No holding hands either. I wanted to ask what was wrong, but I didn't. I waited outside, studied the map of the Gardens: four toilets for ladies, six for gentlemen. Time dragged on. I felt empty. After half an hour of map reading I knew something was wrong. She'd done a runner. Changed her mind. Something I said? Or didn't say? Was she feeling guilty? Thinking of someone else?

Never saw her again.

She might be dead now. Her body buried. Her ashes scattered. But where? But what if she's not? Could I find her?

Should I?

# DOUBLE

I keep feeling I'm being followed shadowed someone looking over my shoulder whispering sharing my memories reading my thoughts back to me my demon? *I'll be your mirror* but I thought that about the therapist and I know I must have been mistaken but now it's so insistent I'm not sure *reflect what you are* unless it's the new medication whose name I still can't pronounce a side effect **special effect** *talking to myself* I've read that it can induce episodes of psychosis paranoia *hearing voices seeing things* although there's nothing about it in the patient information leaflet *unwittingly involved in a mind-manipulating experiment* in the packet *a guinea pig* but they wouldn't tell you *prescription drugs* would they *laced with illegal substances* nor perhaps would the therapist *ketamine* but maybe I should ask her even so always here with you *mephedrone* but maybe it isn't maybe it's something else *lysergic acid diethylamide* perhaps telepathy

there's a blue tit in the tree hopping branch to branch in search of insects it reminded me of a scientist I read once a biologist with an appropriately ornithological name *a type of birdman* Shelduck? **Sheldrake** *Mr Alfred Rupert* conducted tests on telepathy *some say pseudoscientist* but blue tits what's the connection? *Sheltit?* why did that remind me of *Jimi Hendrix* telepathic blue tits? *the lost recordings of The Telepathic Blue Tits* so long now since I read the book starlings too that murmuration I remembered a *colossal formation dance in the sky* all connected somehow must think *not about the individual* flown off now *but the communal* milk bottles that was it *Herman's Hermits* before the War blue tits pecking the foil caps on milk bottles to get at the cream *the bottle stands for love* in a short time blue tits all over were up to it *it seemed a common sight* following the milkmen down the road *a symbol of the dawn* but not by imitation because it spread rapidly further than blue tits travel *a terraced house in a mean street back of town* he called it something **resonance** *not accepted by the mainstream* likewise starlings flocks of thousands before settling to roost perform group aerobatics I saw at Kew intricate manoeuvres without collision as if pre-programmed the flock behaving like a single organism wheeling turning faster than the individual reaction time *like thousands of lads from all over England flocking to Kew* another example of this *intricate manoeuvres to kiss girls at the pagoda* resonance I must reread it *all extremely happy in that particular moment* it's beginning to come back to me *quasi-science some say* morphic was the term *having a specific form or shape* morphic resonance *possibly known as MoRe* a form of memory field

**morphogenetic field** *a hard field* like a magnetic field **organising pattern of influence** *as in a hard disk* *or a cloud server* a collective cumulative memory **memory is inherent in Nature** added to by individual memories *thousands of two-lipped bodies morphing into one glorious kissing mass each encounter a unique endeavour* but also tapped into so as to tune into the memories the thoughts even of others *upload save share* where telepathy fits in **entanglement** *an instinctive desire to mix saliva* but also into our own past memories *one more dose of sweet kissing* saved to the memory bank safe from amnesia safe from decay our moments of happiness *one more time red hot kissing* preserved for retrieval even by others *lips* as in dreams *hot lips* all memories retrievable some painful some pleasant some euphoric but not absurd *say 'kiss my mouth'* now not absurd *'kiss my cheek'* so there's a logical *say 'kiss me'* no teleological? *happy* no *extremely happy theo*logical aspect to it *extremely happy in that moment* released now to *in that particular moment.*

# Junction 11

## Gurnaik Johal & Jon McGregor

In the back seat of your Rover, Jasper Thompson zoomed in on a graph. He mainly seemed concerned with the presentation. He was fiddling with the colour scheme again when more rain landed on the iPad. He shot a look at the other man, Colin, who asked again about the windows.

'They'll steam up,' you said. 'The vents are stuck.' I shrugged at Jasper, sympathetically.

Jasper kept scrolling through the document. Judging by his facial expression, the central narrative of the report was: he was fucked, you were fucked, everyone was fucked.

In the back seat of your Rover, Miles the Authenticator was trying to talk. Something like: *I buffin, peaf. Haf vum humanty, mam.* Even through his gag I could hear his received pronunciation.

We'd cleared the green belt, making good time. We were maybe a half hour from Alia. I made eye contact in the rearview.

*I buffin, tum op! Iff diff joof kenf. Gon ftate froo. Im goana piff myself mam!*

I pulled in at the next lay-by, behind a food truck.

'I'm not a mug, all right?' I said, reaching into the back to

Trees passed. Shredded tyres and body parts on the soft verges. Signs, lighting poles, buckled barriers braced for impact. Sections of pipe left on the side of the road, part of another project that had lost funding, turning green by the side of the road.

'Mistakes have been made,' Jasper began. 'We are human beings.' Colin nodded along. You concentrated on the road. The traffic thinned and you accelerated, the music of passing cars folded into the growing wind, like a radio tuned between stations in old movies. Jasper raised his voice over the noise. 'THE IMPORTANT THING NOW IS TO MOVE ON TOGETHER AND PUT ANY DIVISIONS BEHIND US.'

You eased on to a slip road, towards the services by Junction 11. You were trying not to catch my eye. 'THIS IS NOT THE TIME TO PLAY THE BLAME GAME.' The shouting was unnecessary untie him. 'Don't take me for a mug.'

I pulled out his gag and he gasped, all drama. While he stumbled down into the verge to pee I went up to the truck. I'd not eaten since yours. I left the heating going, it was cold as.

'We're waiting for the AA,' the vendor said. She was dressed the part. Hairnet and everything. 'Nearly out of power but I can just about do you a couple of hot dogs.'

While she cut the buns, I searched for Alia on Find My Friends, my phone on power saver. She was in place with the piece.

I was walking back to the car with the two bratwursts when I realised Miles had done a runner. Not thinking about my Jordans, I followed him into the woods. The trees were young and widely spaced, so he was easy to spot. After two attempts, he cleared a fence and ran out onto a golf now. Colin put a hand to his arm and asked him to take it down a notch. Jasper opened his eyes. 'Why are we stopping? I'm not sure we have time to stop,' he said.

'We need petrol,' you told him.

'How about a coffee, Jasper?' Colin said. 'A latte?'

When the tank was full you parked at the quiet end of the car park. We left them despairing over the presentation in the back of the car and walked across the empty spaces to get the coffees.

'What do they actually do, these ones?' I said, trying not to let on that I recognised Jasper.

You shrugged.

'Politics, right?' I said. 'Or comms? Political communications?'

You told me again that a key company policy was not to ask questions of, or about, clients. I decided not to push it. I was only in the car today because the job was one way and you'd offered me the ride. My father lived on the south coast, and the task of putting his affairs

course, his Oxfords squeaking with dew. I clipped his ankles and he tumbled into a bunker.

'Man,' I said, sitting next to him in the sand.

'I don't know who you are or where you're taking me.'

'I told you it's not deep. A meeting. An opportunity.'

'You had me gagged.'

'You were kicking up a fuss. I didn't want it to come to that.'

'And you just happened to have zip ties handy?'

'It was a last resort.'

'I'm not moving until you tell me everything. I'll scream, honest, I'll—'

'All right, Jesus. Ketchup or mustard?' I handed him his hot dog and showed him a picture of the piece on my phone.

Miles had first seen the piece last month. Alia had taken it to his office for forensic scans. It was a Ruiz, an artist who'd sold a few dozen portraits in her short lifetime. After her death, several more in order had fallen, somehow, to me. *Had* lived. He *had* lived on the south coast. The trains were still not running. I'd long given up my car. You said you could take a few days off the app once you'd dropped these clients off. That you'd be there for me, if it got weird. It was the *being there for me* that I was starting to find weird, to be honest.

When we returned with the coffees, the car was empty. The clients had disappeared. You swore softly.

'Is there a company policy about losing your customers?'

'It's not funny. Let's split up.'

You searched the car park, checked the app, made calls. I went back into the building, scanning the food court and the shops. I loitered outside the toilets. You appeared as I was circling the arcade machines for a second time. Nothing. We headed back to the car. My phone was nearly dead, and I plugged it in to charge from the lighter socket. You checked your phone for messages or works had surfaced, apparently dug out by friends, setting auction houses alight. They were later deemed forgeries, and O'Hagan, the artist responsible, was imprisoned in a trial that made the news. O'Hagan's pieces dipped and then rose in value, sparking a new wave of lesser forgeries. People were selling Ruiz's work, O'Hagan's forgeries of her work and knockoffs of those knockoffs, which is where Miles the Authenticator, biting into his bratwurst, came in.

'God, I needed this.'

He was compiling the world's first Ruiz/O'Hagan catalogue raisonné and had categorised Alia's piece as a fake. In that one email she'd lost a hundred grand, which included the money she owed me, and, I suppose, with how things are going, the money I now owe you.

'We just wanted you to come to the table, is all,' I said, emptying sand from my Ones.

updates, but there was nothing. The coffee was awful; they'd messed up the order and I was pretty sure mine wasn't even decaf. It was raining again. I looked out at the muddy ground around the picnic tables and saw footprints, heading into a tangled copse of thorny trees.

'Are those new footprints, do you think?' We both looked at them for a moment. 'Should we go and find them?'

'We should stay with the car,' you said. I remembered your hesitancy to ever get muddy when we were kids, how you cried one time when I made you climb a tree. How your dad hadn't known which of us to be cross with. It was uncomfortable, sometimes, remembering us as children. Given where we were now. It made the whole thing kind of unsavoury.

'I'll go,' I said. I stepped out of the car and ditched the coffee.

The tracks grew fainter as the tree cover got denser. I tried to read the broken twigs and swaying branches

'You drive me home, we draw a line under it. Done. I'll tell no one.'

We started to make our way back off the golf course towards your car. Alia was supposed to do the talking, but I couldn't let the opportunity go. 'We're offering 10 percent,' I said. 'You say it's real art. We cash out, you take your cut. Everyone wins.'

The food truck came into view, the road quiet.

'This day,' Miles said. 'This day!'

It took me a moment to catch up. Your car was gone. I may or may not have left the keys in the ignition. The hotdog vendor had vanished, leaving her broken-down van behind.

'There's no Uber,' I said on the phone to Alia. 'No Bolt.'

Miles paced.

'I've got no data,' I said. 'Can't you figure out a taxi company or something?'

the way a Girl Guide might do. Or a hunter. I strained to hear their voices – they surely couldn't have got far – but could only hear the sound of water or the wind in the trees or the motorway. I remembered that when you'd got stuck up the tree your dad had looked scared of going to get you, but that he'd gone anyway. The mossy scuffs on his polished shoes when he'd come back down, and the smear of sweat across his face. The way he'd tried to hide his pride.

When we'd first got together, officially, I'd always liked spending time at your parents' house. It made me feel a part of things.

When the doctor had reached me with the news of my father's death, she'd asked me to confirm his identity over the phone. I said I wasn't sure I could be considered the next of kin. I asked how she'd even got my number. Surely, after all these years, there'd be someone else. The doctor switched to video-call, and said: so?

Miles and I searched for a sign. I was reading out the name of the golf course when my phone died. Yes, if fingers were to be pointed, I'd taken Miles' phone when I picked him up, attaching it to your dashboard to use for directions and save my battery.

'This is quite the situation we're in,' Miles said, pointing at me. 'Quite the bloody situation.'

I opened the back door to the abandoned food-truck and turned on the hob to warm my hands.

'We wait?' Miles said, appearing on the other side of the service hatch, 'that's all you've got?'

When the AA van arrived, Angela the Mechanic took a while to catch up on the facts.

'This isn't your food-truck. You have no keys.'

'Right.'

'You're not an AA priority member, and you didn't call us.'

'No, but—'

'And your car's been stolen.'

'Exactly.'

He was sitting up in an armchair, which was the first surprise. I'd expected a hospital bed, a trolley in a morgue, a white sheet being pulled back. But he was right there: lolling in an armchair, head tipped to one side, mouth hanging open. He had the same nose as me, a pair of glasses slipping forward. The same way mine always do. She tilted the phone down to show me his hands folded over a book in his lap; and up, to his face, his head, his hair a tangled nest.

~

The doctor ended the call and filled out the forms. There were messages from home, and her phone started ringing again. She left the paperwork at reception and rushed out through the rain to the bus.

'Did the sandbags arrive?' she asked, when she got through on the phone. 'Insurance said it would be today.' The connection wavered. 'Well, make do with the towels. *The towels.*'

'Well, you better hop in.'

Angela agreed to drive us to the next town over, where we could wait in the warmth.

'If you need to make any calls,' she said, nodding at the phone in the holder.

'Could you pass it?' Miles said to me. I was all out of road. I handed over the phone. Miles paused at the keypad, dappled in the speckled shadows of bird shit the wipers couldn't reach. He put the phone to his ear and shook his head, his hair a tangled nest.

~

'Look, we talk this over, or we go to the police,' Miles said. I smiled at Angela, maintaining a tense pose of outward calm, like all those times I'd sat for Alia, unable to move because she refused to paint from stills. It wasn't my sort of thing, lying naked in that draughty studio, but she promised that my face wouldn't be used, promised good money – 'it's nothing I haven't seen before.' Only

On the bus, she swiped through her feed, watching a video of Jasper Thompson caught in a scrum of journalists as he returned home from a jog. Someone had looped the clip of him running and set it to a synth-heavy 1980s duet, superimposing him on a variety of backgrounds: pulling out ahead of Bolt in the 100m finals, running up the steps with Rocky, on the beach with the Chariots of Fire lads.

Colin had rewatched the video several times before omitting it from Jasper's media roundup. He thought of it now as Jasper ran on ahead into the dismal woods, finally losing steam.

'Can we be serious, Jasper?' he said. 'I've been told not to overexert.'

'I am serious, Colin. We can disappear. The two of us. Make a life for ourselves out here in the woods. Go off the grid. I'll set traps, hunt squirrels. You were always talking about fishing

one of her promises came true – she superimposed someone else's face over mine on every canvas: men, women, vacant expressions.

'You have my Monzo,' I said, when I came to view the finished pieces. I was in the red after a series of bad investments and had just gone all-in on a pair of Off-Whites on StockX that turned out to be fugazi. 'I sent a request. You said end of the month.' By way of a reply, she showed me the Ruiz – her inheritance.

'You've been having a bad day,' Miles said on the phone. 'I understand that. So have I, to be honest with you. Yes. Yes, I know. But listen. You're no thief. I'm not using names. No. You just needed a way out. I get that.'

Was he talking to the hot dog lady? He was. It took me several turns to realise the number would have been in Angela's recent calls. He moved the phone away from his ear and started asking Angela about service stations.

with your old man. Wasn't he a hippie?'

'He had an alternative world-view.' They both stopped. 'We can discuss this in the car. In the warmth.'

Jasper pushed on through the trees, and disappeared. Colin tried calling the driver, but there was no answer. He called the office instead.

'Just stepped out for a quick scrum on a comms issue. Nothing like fresh air for blue sky thinking. But listen, we might have a situation with the Minister?'

He listened, and nodded.

'Where are we? It's a good question. Okay. Well, we're in some woods.'

He'd lost sight of Jasper. He'd got himself turned around while he'd been on the call, and he didn't know which way to follow. He heard the snapping of twigs, and something that might have been the rushing sound of water.

'Ah. Okay. I'll call you when I find him.'

'We'll meet at Junction 11 Services. Okay. By the picnic area. And just walk away. Lovely Ang will meet you by Starbucks. Yes, AA. She'll get you sorted out. This is for the best. You don't want to get mixed up with these people. Okay? Okay. Bye now. Bye. Bye.'

Miles looked straight ahead, the wide concrete judder of the motorway rolling beneath the AA truck's wheels and the sky opening out before us.

'Fifty percent,' he said.

I nodded.

Angela dropped us off at the services and we walked to the far end of the car park. As discussed, your car was parked by the picnic benches. The keys were in the ignition and I spared no time. I put my phone on charge and drove on. Your heating was finally working properly, and merging with the motorway, things were getting back on track. Even Miles, sitting next to me, looked relaxed. He turned the radio on and raised the

A few days after the doctor had put me on the video call with my dead dad, I got a call from a hospital. They were following up about a screening. My father's condition was hereditary, they said, but they could catch it early. A camera would be inserted, snaking through me. I remembered a cartoon I'd watched as a kid, the characters shrinking down to the size of bugs and jumping into their dad's ear canal, swimming through the channels of his brain, down into his arteries and intestines, swirling around through his lungs before being sneezed out through his nose and back into their non-dad lives.

The scrub and the tangles of plastic got denser and the sound of the motorway faded away. I didn't seem any closer to finding either Jasper or the other guy. My hair kept snagging in brambles and there was an increasingly sewage-like smell underfoot. I was just about to give up and turn back when I broke through

volume. It wasn't my kind of thing, he must have switched the stations.

'Takes me back to—'

'Who the fuck are you?'

There was a man in the back of the car. We met each other's gaze in the rearview. There was a man in the back of your car.

'What is happening?' the man said. 'Where's Colin? The other two? Who are you?'

'Who are you more like?'

'Jasper—'

This was not your car. The air freshener was green, not blue. The fuel tank was full, yours was close to empty. There hadn't been a phone charger in your car.

'There, uh, seems to be some kind of a misunderstanding,' I began.

The man was panicking. 'I'll call the police. Who are you with? PETA? Greta? This a ransom thing? Tree-hug fucks. Because I will prosecute. I'll come for you, I'll come—'

Miles removed his wedding ring and punched the man in

into a clearing. It turned out to be the same stretch of car-park and picnic benches I thought I'd left behind. You were gone. Your car was gone. From a passing van I heard Freddie Mercury singing about being under pressure before giving up completely and just going um ba ba be.

~

Colin was sitting on a picnic bench, talking into his phone. He looked at me, blankly at first and then with suspicion. The expression on a schoolteacher's face when you see them some years after leaving school, in a pub. The feeling that they should know you, but that they shouldn't be there, or you shouldn't be there, or they shouldn't acknowledge you.

Your Rover was gone. My hand went to my pocket before I remembered leaving my phone in your car, charging. I wondered what had been so urgent that you would have left like that, leaving the face. Other drivers passed in snatches. I risked a glance back, the stowaway was out cold. Miles climbed into the back to tie the man's hands. 'It's sixty percent,' Miles said. 'You hear?'

The singer on the radio kept going, 'um ba ba be,' and I turned the music off.

~

'Where am I going?' I asked Miles. 'What am I doing?'

'Get off at the next junction and turn around. We'll drop him back at the services, and then go on to your friend. You'll take me back to the office, with the piece. I'll do my scans, your friend will take it to auction by the end of the month, the money will come through not long after, we split ways, never talk about any of this again. It'll be like it never happened.'

'I need to find the real car.'

I indicated towards Junction 12 and turned back the way we had come.

Miles had taken the man's phone out of his pocket and, pulling the

95

me behind. I wondered what I was to you, really, that you would do that. I wondered if you were coming back.

Colin had ended his conversation and was just looking at his phone, not touching it. I moved closer, waiting for him to look up.

'Can I use your phone?'

'Where's the driver?'

'Yeah, I mean, I guess he's in the car?'

'So where's the car, I'm asking. What kind of car service is this?'

'Well where's your guy? You're the ones who disappeared first.'

'We had things to discuss.'

'Right. Well, my phone's in the car. So could I use yours, sort this out?'

'Well. Sure. I can make the call for you.'

'Mate, I'm not going to steal your phone.'

'Security protocols. There's a lot of information on this phone. What's the number? I'll put it on speaker.'

'Really? Bloody hell.'

man's gag down, unlocked it with face recognition. He called a recent number, and put it on loudspeaker. A woman. The owner of this Rover.

While he arranged a second rendezvous, my phone came to life by the gear stick. Messages from Alia stacked up, covering the photo of your shadow I took that day by the lake. There was an Instagram notification from you, too – yes, I have an alert on for your posts. Rejoining the queue at Junction 11, I pressed it.

'Jan dump' was a series of photos from last month, candids of friends at New Year's, your niece at the park, a bottomless brunch, and then, in the last image, there was me, or part of me. It was a mirror-selfie you'd taken on our first trip together. My right shoulder and arm were visible towards the edge of the frame. It was my first time on your grid. I'd been soft-launched.

I didn't know what to do with the information, it seemed to belong to a different life, the two of us in front of that mirror, in the hotel room, a

96

I didn't know your number. No-one knows people's numbers anymore. I gave him mine instead, hoping that if you saw my phone ringing on the dashboard you'd pick it up.

Colin and I sat on the picnic bench, in the rain, and listened to my phone ring out and go to voicemail. I left a message, telling you what we both already knew.

'Right then,' Colin said. 'Here we go. They're back.'

Your Rover came edging across the car park again, and pulled up. Someone else got out of the driver's seat, putting up her hands apologetically. She looked like she worked in Gregg's. Hairnet and everything.

'Which one of you is Miles?'

We looked at her. Her question made so little sense that neither of us could speak.

'Right, of course. Look, I'm sorry, okay? I didn't mean to – it was a misunderstanding, right?

different world. When we checked into the hotel, we said we were half-brothers. The receptionist said we looked like twins, which made us both cringe. We joked about it as we drifted through the Old Town – were we both narcissists? – going from checkpoint to checkpoint, café to restaurant, restaurant to gallery, gallery to bar – where you put your hand on my thigh – bar to church. We couldn't read the signage next to the church door. You'd read a blog that said the stained glass shouldn't be missed so we opened it, stepping into the middle of a child's baptism. Everyone inside turned to look. The priest carrying out the ceremony walked quickly towards us, his footsteps echoing, water dripping on the cold tiles. We stepped back, closed the door and laughed.

'We're going to hell.'

'We were always going to hell.'

We returned to the hotel and found the twin beds that we'd pushed together had been pulled apart again by the cleaner.

Look, anyway, here it is. Let's just draw a line.'

I looked at the car and wondered where you'd gone this time. I was very, very tired. I didn't want to go and put my father's affairs in order anymore. I didn't want to go anywhere. The man had never bothered putting his own affairs in order. What difference would it make if I was to do it now?

'Hello? Can we go?' Colin was up and at the car already, pulling at the back door.

'Colin! Mate! Pay attention, will you? Your driver's not here. Your boss is not here. Where are you going?'

'I'm going to make some calls. I'll be in the car.'

I watched him get into the back seat. I waited for the penny to drop. He sat there, in the back of the wrong car, looking at his phone and not making any calls at all. I wondered what weird parallel series of events had ended up with this car here in front of us and your

As a joke, we lay in our separate beds, but you were so tired you actually fell asleep. I scrolled through the news, workers on a controversial pipeline had dug up two parallel graves, in what archaeologists claimed was a site of importance. There was a theory going around that the bodies had been recently buried on the pipeline's proposed route as a ruse to halt progress. The story reminded me of the time capsule that we dug up in year 6, which contained a letter from a Victorian child, one of their old teddy bears and a pair of their shoes. If Alia didn't have a younger sister who also went to our school, I would never have known that at the end of the school year our teacher would rebury the capsule to use again next term. Alia had met the teacher at the pub once, and called her up on it. She said she'd had to fabricate a lie, it brought the subject to life.

Alia used the story for a series she called 'Capture'. She got her friends to lend her items of car somewhere else entirely. I wondered where you were, and whether I would make it to the south coast at all. I tried to remember the last time I'd seen my father, the rigid brace of his shoulders from the back seat of his car, the hunched way he pushed his fury into his driving, swinging into corners and lurching through gaps in the traffic that were barely even there, telling my mother to shut up shut up just shut up every time she asked him to please, please slow down. The sticky hot vinyl of the back seat against my bare legs. The smell of travel sweets. The sweet wrappers stuffed into the netting on the back of the driver's seat. The burning rubber smell of the damage he was doing.

I tried to remember if he'd even said goodbye when he left. If there was a single moment when he was definitively leaving, or if the gaps between the times he came back just merged into one

sentimental value and then she 3D-printed plastic replicas of them. The pieces found no buyers and remained in boxes in the studio. Somewhere in one of the boxes were the Air Forces I'd given her which she never returned. You always zoned out when I talked about shoes, which was why, in bed this morning, I'd asked to use your car to go and sell one of my limited editions.

'You know those deadstock Yeezys? Someone's agreed to buy them, can I borrow the car to deliver them? We agreed to meet halfway.'

I played the moment over in my head, imagining a parallel universe where you'd refused and I'd avoided all this mess.


'Mate, I think we might need to take two for a quick scrum,' Miles said, climbing into the front. He'd been going through the man's phone. 'He's a fucking minister.'

'A priest?'

'They could try us for, I don't know, treason, terrorism. This isn't funny.'

long absence. I was too young to remember for sure. It was too late to ask my mum.

He'd taken the car with him when he left, I know that. It was a long time before Mum had a car of her own. I associated cars with men for years; the look and the smell of them, the driving of them, the being stuck in a passenger seat while a man drives in a way that makes you uncomfortable or unwell or fearful for your own safety or survival, the relishing of your fear and discomfort, the habitual need to just be in complete fucking control all the fucking time.

Put your own affairs in fucking order, you dead fuck, is mostly what I was thinking by then.

I got into the driver's seat. Colin was holding his phone in his lap, staring straight ahead.

'You not making any calls?'

'Battery's dead. What a day.'

'We'll head off, will we?'

'Your boyfriend's not coming back then?'

'Wasn't me who punched him.'

'You're an accomplice. An accessory, whatever it is. We're in this together.'

We looked back at the minister.

'When we get to the roundabout we're going to need to keep driving.'

'But I need to get my boyfriend's car.' It came out just like that: *boyfriend*.

'We can't be seen with him at the services. There's cameras everywhere.'

'It's all he has left of his dad.'

'There's probably police waiting for us already.'

'They did it up together. The whole car. Two summers.'

'I suggest you do as I say, because if we were to be forced to explain how we got here I'd have to describe you bundling me into your car, your boyfriend's car, sorry, and bringing me here.'

The gap in the traffic opened and I joined the Junction 11 roundabout. I drove round twice before following Miles'

'Is yours?'

'Funny. He's my boss, actually. You're the back-up driver then, are you?'

'I'm a driver.'

'Okay, great. Yes, let's go. You have a charger up there?'

'Colin, I've never seen this car before, how would I know?'

'You've never seen – what? This isn't the same car?'

'Buckle up.'

My driving was tentative through the car parks and exit lanes. Other cars kept backing into view suddenly, performing confident three-point turns. Children appeared on faded zebra crossings, looking at the sky. At the end of the parking bays, merging with the lanes for the petrol station, I glanced in my rear-view mirror and saw you standing in the road. You were holding two fresh coffees, and although I couldn't see your face there was the suggestion of confusion in the way you held yourself. I thought about

instructions, off along an A road, towards the woods. Eventually, I turned down a narrow lane, and we dumped the man and his iPad at the edge of some national park. I tossed him a water bottle and turned the car around. We continued down the country lanes until we reached a river. I parked the car to the side of the bridge, and waited for Alia to arrive. I turned the radio on, then off. When Alia's hatchback arrived, we got in and I tossed the Rover's keys into the water.

'To catch you up,' I said, sitting in the back with Miles. 'We agreed 60/40.'

'Oh,' she said.

'That's 60 me, 40 you,' Miles said.

'So, 20/20 me and you,' I added.

'Not being funny, that's not on. I own the artwork. I make the numbers.'

'You can't sell it without me.'

'If I happen to mention that you're willing to bend the rules about what you deem real,' Alia stopping, but I didn't think about it for long. In truth I didn't like the way you drove. I no longer trusted you behind the wheel of a car.

We hit the motorway, and I started to enjoy myself. Cars had come on a long way since the last time I'd driven one, clearly, and this one had a very smooth and responsive acceleration. I soon moved into the fast lane, and mostly stayed there. The road seemed to climb and keep climbing, and the fields beside the road sloped away all gold with wheat and sunshine. There were bridges, and gantries, and junctions that spun off into complications, but mostly there was this light and the sensation of light falling upon us, the swish swish swish of passing metalwork and the rumble of the tyres beneath us.

'Sorry, could you? There's no time pressure here. If you could slow down a little?'

'Can't hear you, Colin. Sit back please.'

said, 'I think you might find yourself out of a job.'

'How about 50/50 between all of us,' I said. '33/33/33.'

'I can do 50/50 if you want it to be an O'Hagan. But for a Ruiz, I'm putting my career on the line. My name. 60/40.'

When we arrived at Miles' office, I asked him to punch me. The windows were steaming up.

'I'm sorry?'

'Look, I've lost my boyfriend's car. So I'm going to have to explain how that happened. But I can't exactly use the truth.'

'Why not?'

'That would involve telling him I'm owed money by my ex-girlfriend, money I'm owed because I've been modelling for her nudes.'

'Sitting.'

'But how is a punch going to help?'

'He thinks I've taken his car to sell a pair of trainers – look, it's a long story – but I can say I was

We passed white vans and tow trucks, mini-buses and coaches, saloons and hatchbacks and SUVs, supermarket delivery vans and logistics lorries and a mobile home on the back of a trailer. A minibus with blacked out windows and the branding of a private school painted across the side. Another minibus with a cross painted on the back door and the name of a Baptist ministry signwritten in 3D letters. As we started to pass the church minibus it drifted into our lane. I sounded the horn and it jerked back away from us. As we cruised smoothly past the driver gestured towards me and made angry shapes with his mouth. He was wearing a dog collar and it didn't look like the words he was saying were becoming of a minister. I ignored him and drove on, and in the rearview mirror I saw him swing into the fast lane behind us.

In the back seat Colin was watching me silently. I wondered where he thought we were going. I wondered where Jasper had got to, and

attacked by the customer. They hit me, took the shoes, stole the car. It's a narrative.'

'Right,' Miles said, removing his wedding ring.

'You can come back to mine,' Alia said. 'Only because it's closer.'

'I'm okay.'

'So you two are official, then.'

'I wouldn't say that.'

'You used "boyfriend".'

'It's just here on the right.'

You weren't home when she dropped me off. I was going to let myself in when I realised that if I'd been mugged, I probably wouldn't have all my things. I dug a small hole beneath your struggling hydrangea and buried my phone and wallet and your keys.

You returned a few minutes later.

'I got an alert from the doorbell,' you said, 'what are you doing? What happened to your face?'

You opened the door, but didn't follow me in. I watched

103

what would be happening to the graphs and reports the two of them had been working on. I wondered what would happen to my father, his head tipped back in that armchair, with no-one to put his affairs in order. Would they just close the door and leave him there?

The light falls from the day and the road rises on ahead of us. My mother knew what she was doing when she left my father behind. I knew what I was doing when I left you in the car park, the two coffees held stupidly in your hands. Jasper knew what he was doing when he ran off into the woods. There is fuel in the tank enough to get us somewhere better than this. I am driving too fast and I love it. That Baptist guy keeps getting closer.

you unearth my things through the living room window. It was deeply humiliating, so unlike you to use your hands.

The light shifted as I looked, the window acting as a mirror. My face didn't look real, didn't belong to me: the blood dried impasto on the pastel blue and purple hues of a blooming bruise. You washed your hands and found the first aid kit. I rested my head on your lap and looked up at you looking down. You were breaking out. Thinking it was over and that I had nothing else to lose, I told you the truth, all this, and you let me lie there, still, until I drifted off, opening different doors in my sleep – the car, the bedroom, the church – walking, now running, as that Baptist guy keeps getting closer.

# The Backyard of Fuck Around and Find Out

Anna Cowling & Ruby Wood

*To Jorge Luis Borges*

On page 121 of his since-discredited smash-hit book *Why We Fight: A Taxonomy of Argument from Tiff to Terrorism* (2035), 'Dr' James Pryce claims that a coordinated piece scheduled to appear in three British tabloids (and supported by a pre-planned and astroturfed social media campaign) against an 'extremely high-profile' public figure, scheduled for 2 October 2028, had to be pulled at the very last minute. One of Pryce's characteristically lengthy paragraphs describes the legal basis for the superinjunction that caused the sudden rush to stop the press – a moment of industrial drama which lacked any particular repercussions for the three newspapers in question except that it forced each of them to run transparently scanty and frankly uninteresting front pages the next day.

The following account throws new light on certain side details of this event. The text was found on a USB stick dropped under a seat on a Jubilee line train and retrieved by a cleaner working his last shift at the Stanmore depot, and appears to have been written by an Amber Rooney – though this is almost undoubtedly a false name. The author further signed themself Actor / Model / Friend / Mistake-Maker / Forgiveness-Seeker / Comeback Queen.

An unknown number of the opening pages were corrupted by damage to the USB stick, thought to have been caused by the cleaner's 11-month-old son.

~

...so I switched it to silent and ignored it, or tried to. I remembered our first meeting, how we became the centre of the room, for once, the boys orbiting around us. Now just a few months later we were in a different universe, me and my Ella, and I didn't feel sad about that first meeting and everything we'd lost since then – our lives battered beyond recognition, and where are those we should blame? Who will make them pay? Before I go to bed tonight, I said to myself, I will destroy those dogs, those vermin.[1] One way or another, I'll get it done. And after that, I'll be ready to speak to her. I'll call her and, once it's all sorted, she'll be relieved, she'll have no need to try to convince me of other

---

1 This language may seem dramatic, but with hindsight it can be said with some confidence that the repercussions of the actions outlined in this account were not insignificantly violent, and surprisingly far-reaching. Whether the original intentions of the author went as far as implied here will, however, be a matter for eternal debate. – *Note by the manuscript editors*

possibilities. She has to be loyal, you see, she has to feel good about herself that way. It's a weakness really but an endearing one, most of the time. So I'll do what I have to do and she'll be relieved, she'll welcome the freedom, and the drama. Let's not pretend she won't fucking love the drama.

The only room with a lock on the door is my little bathroom – it's where I always go when I need space around me to think, even though shutting myself into some cool inner chamber seems ridiculous when there's no one else in. I stepped over the edge of the empty bathtub and lay in it. I like that hard enamel, the cool that seeps slowly through my clothes. Same old view through the skylight: a few gutters, a few last leaves clinging on. Out of nowhere this was going to be the day of my revenge – and I could feel something coming, like a swelling, like a laugh that might overwhelm me completely if I let it, when I thought about how long we'd waited for it and how suddenly it had come. For some reason my mum came into my mind, the street I grew up on, everything that happened back then, and I thought: look at me.

I thought about how things keep on happening, keep on happening to me and to you, *now* and *now* and *now*. Second follows second, day follows day, and weeks and years and centuries and EPOCHS, and we are forever stuck in the present. Stuck together, now. And if it's happening to you, isn't it happening to me too? And to all of us. I was considering all of this, like turning a knot round and round in my hands, when that picture of my mum's soft face emerged again and pulled me back to the cool enamel.

While I lay there, in a weird sort of pumped-up trance (now that I can see what that was, now that I understand everything that was going on, and I know it's pointless trying to hark back to a time when there was someone looking out for me), even though I was completely psyched I couldn't forget that she, my languorous and mood-led beauty, was still clueless about the Hand Grenade – that hard, undeniable proof of what the prime minister had been doing and just how many people it had harmed. Right now I was the only one who knew. A flurry of leaves blew past the skylight then, and in my mind they were the shreds and tatters of his reputation, the thin layers of his ego finally blown apart. But I needed to make sure I was believed – that the evidence I had would reach the right person's screen at the right moment. I'd been undercover so long I'd succeeded in becoming nobody (to all the world, except to her). None of my channels were secure. HQ didn't give a shit, I'd realised years ago – you could give them something on a Big Name and they'd act all serious and grateful, and as if you were a crucial asset, then they'd literally just chuck the intel in the bin and leave you to freeze. Yet the Hand Grenade had to be thrown, and fast. And she'd see it happening and she'd know. I said out loud, 'fuck it. Let's go.'

I sat up in the bath, abrupt and erect like Nosferatu, in lucid and lovely silence, as if it had already happened, as if it was already done. Something – a kind of nosiness that I was directing, illogically, at myself – made me empty out my pockets. I felt I was examining evidence. The newest iPhone, in red; the keys to our house with the seashell keyring

Jenny had made; a receipt from the chemist's (paid in cash); six twenties, a tenner, some pound coins and shrapnel; a scribbled note which I decided to destroy at once (and which I did not destroy); and my folding knife with the corkscrew.

The whole plan took me less than ten minutes to put together. I already had a catalytic object in mind: Maria Ripples-Kismet, a rather chic old-school journalist whose path I'd crossed once or twice (or possibly a lot more often than that), though each time briefly, and usually in disguise. One quick Google and I knew where to find her. It was an address near Gilkestead, less than an hour away.

The thing is, I am a brave woman. I can say it now, now that I have brought my incredibly risky plan to an end. It was not easy. The details were unexpected but the execution was perfect, and I fucking did it. Not for the glory, or for the money. I used to believe I did it for her, for Ella, but I've known women like her all my life, the most magnificent events on god's green earth. I am them, and I long to be them.

But also, I carried out my plan, let's face it, because the boss had underestimated me too many times. (Deep down a misogynist, like so many who spout loudly about their belief in women's rights.) One of my flaws is that I can't let go of the need to prove myself. And there in that moment I had to move. I had this feeling someone was coming for me. My phone, on silent, sitting there like a bomb.

I got dressed, and I looked fabulous. The street was quiet while I waited for my taxi, but I imagined people could see me, were watching me, appreciating me. I could have walked to the station but that felt too low-rent, and too vulnerable if I'm honest. I didn't actually want anyone to see me. I told the driver to drop me round the corner from the main entrance and I emerged from that taxi like a fresh powerful breeze.

I was heading to Okeham, a speck of a village that didn't even materialise until I zoomed right in on the map. The train that would get me vaguely close to it was already there on the platform, but it wasn't due to leave until 19:51 – still ten minutes away, so I strolled up the stairs and crossed the bridge without rushing. It was nice and quiet. I walked through the carriages. I remember some tall, shaggy-haired lads in school uniform, a woman dressed like she was going to a wedding, a youth deep in Carlo Rovelli's *Helgoland* and a genial-looking old man with crutches.

When the train finally started moving, a man I knew well ran furiously and pointlessly along the platform. It was that little Westminster sewer rat John Morrey. The doors lock one minute before departure, dickhead. I smiled at him but I don't think he saw me. The timing was so exquisite, it was erotic.

From this little rush of euphoria I gradually drifted into a sort of soporific bliss. The fight had already started – and here I was, easy winner of round one. That bastard would be waiting on the platform for an hour now, as I hurtled further and further away from him; an almost literal sliding-doors moment, sure, but didn't that intervention of fate somehow support what I was doing? The auto-locking doors weren't human-operated, were they, so that meant other forces had to be on my side, keeping me free, keeping me alive. And so alive! This bliss I felt just underlined how fucking unbeatable

I was. They thought they'd be able to keep us down, but they never would, now – I was sure of it.

I've watched us all put up with considerably too much shit, day in day out, sinking drowning gasping kicking at nothing, bugs on a pin, while the vandals and the bandits thrive and laugh. So let me tell you what I know: *you fight like you're already dead.* Or, perhaps this would look better on Instagram: *you fight like you've already won.*

And that's what I did, while my heart seemed to beat in some future place, feeling as if it had already been through all the sudden speedings and recoveries of what was to come, and I watched as the greyish light slid away from the day.

The train stopped and started and whooshed and chugged for half an hour or so, through suburbs, past playgrounds, an industrial estate, forlorn trees. Every moment felt as clear and bright as the last. The train slowed and stopped, basically in the middle of a field. There was no station announcement. 'Okeham?' I asked some kids on the platform. 'Okeham,' they replied. I got out.

The kids were crowded around one of their phones, watching something, which meant they were weirdly lit from below – I could hardly see their faces. But one of them broke off and said: 'are you off to that big mansion? With the hippies?' His voice was serious, curious. I'd barely opened my mouth before another, the smallest, said: 'it's miles. But you won't get lost if you take the road to the left and then go left again whenever you've got a choice.' I wanted to give them something for helping me, but what? I just smiled my thanks. They'd gone back to their video anyway.

Out of the station, I went left along a deserted road. I followed its long, shallow bend and it began going downhill. It was a plain dirt way, no lights or markings, with branches intermingling above me as if to encourage my path. Not far above the horizon there was a big full moon, hanging there, saying: *I see you – yep, it's you and me, babe*.

For a second I thought John Morrey might somehow know what I was up to, might know where I'd got off, might ask those kids. But I knew it wouldn't happen, the man's a dunce, plus remember I was already dead. The kids' advice to turn left whenever I could reminded me of what my mum had told me, and her mum had told her – it is the most common way to find the middle of a maze. Not for nothing am I the grandchild of Julia Ward. She was head gardener at Elsenbury, a revered and much desired figure among her esoteric circles, a woman in a man's world, of course, who designed the best hornbeam and hazel mazes in the west, and wrote a now-lost book of romantic poetry which, family lore has it, was buried at the centre of her favourite maze. Fragments remain, notes she made, and they glow with molten beauty. Julia died in her fifties, too young too young, in circumstances which were not so much suspicious as absolutely stinking.

Under the all-seeing eye of that moon I thought about Julia: the way she loved words and the living narratives that are forests, her written legacy that may or may not be buried as the family story goes. Wouldn't she have kept a copy somewhere? Maybe it had existed but, underground, had long ago rotted down to a damp brick. Maybe there was never a book. Or maybe – maybe – it was a work so brilliant, so dangerous, that it scared her. She'd known instinctively the trouble that would come down on her if the world got hold of it, with all its transgressions, its blinding experiments, its mind-blowingly intertwined references back to her work with the mazes. That's what I pictured (what I knew, somehow, and always had): she'd written something that went beyond the normal, something that blew apart the constricted, linear, so-called visions of her contemporaries and instead referred outward and inward at the same time; calling to dimensions they couldn't even conceive. Something that took in both past and future and somehow involved the stars.

For the first time that day, lost in ancestral vertigo, I forgot my plan. For a few minutes, maybe, I was not of this world. I was special, a spectre. The dull little roads I walked down seemed incredible, my friend the moon, the steady lurch of the evening, it all stirred something within me. Going down the gently sloping road in the just-beyond-dusk, my resolve became diamond-hard while my options suddenly sprang open: glorious, heady multiples, spinning themselves into a tapestry. I was everywhere, and gone.

I kept on, down the hill, down still. The road kept branching off, and took me between fields with that late-evening mist rising off them. I could hear something, too: a kind of music on the air. Little snatches of treble, beats that came and went from a way away, softened through the trees.

I thought about how a woman might be the enemy of other women, of the varied incarnations of other women, of the versions of herself even, but she is never the enemy of a place: not of fireflies, words, gardens, music, or the stillness of an evening.

Lost in enjoyment of these thoughts, I was surprised when I suddenly came up against a tall, crisply painted black gate. Through the railings I could see one of those gorgeous avenues, a wide, soft curve with poplars every few metres – a real period-drama cliché – and a sort of pavilion. The music I'd been hearing was coming from there. Then it suddenly hit me: it was our song. *You can stand under my umbrella*. That was why I'd carried on with such a warm, steady feeling inside, down and down the long hill.

I rang the bell.

It was a pretty fucking impressive place for a journalist, even a chic and well-connected one. From the end of the avenue, from the main house, a light approached; the cold light from a phone, which swung and tottered, illuminated bits of fancy brickwork on the path, disappeared for moments behind tree trunks. I couldn't see the person behind it, but they approached in a hurry, with purpose, you know?

Maria Ripples-Kismet opened the gate and spoke slowly, in a gentle voice that made me lean in.

'I see you've troubled yourself to come all this way,' she said. Sarcastic, I think. 'No doubt you want to see the garden.'

My skin, my blood, everything prickled. 'The garden?'

'The garden of consequential choices.'

I hadn't known until that moment, but suddenly I did. Everything I was here to do suddenly gained an extra layer of inevitability – and of justification. I said, not caring that I was completely blowing my cover: 'that's my gran's garden. My grandma, Julia Ward.'

'You're Julia Ward's granddaughter? Well, come in.'

The damp path zigzagged like those of my childhood. When we reached the house, we went into a kitchen filled with roses, hydrangeas, other flowers I didn't quite recognise, clusters of pink and blue and yellow. There were piles of papers, too – mostly handwritten, some printed, some tucked inside coloured paper folders, not quite chaotic. The radio was on, but the song had changed. I remember a jar of pennies, and a cat was sitting by the sink, watching me.

Maria was watching me too, but, same as the cat, her face wasn't giving much away. She was what they used to call a handsome woman, well-dressed. She had great skin and large grey eyes. Her physical presence made you feel you could trust her – maybe that's what had got her so far in the world of spads, snakes and shifting allegiances.

I perched on a stool at the kitchen counter, and she leaned back, a bit louche really, next to her cat. I was thinking about John Morrey, whether he'd be on his way yet. We might only have an hour. But then an hour can be a long, long time. The Hand Grenade, my propelling force a few hours ago, was half-forgotten, just a silly USB stick. My intentions seemed to have splintered.

'Funny thing about your grandmother,' said Ripples-Kismet, more or less out of nowhere. 'The famous Julia Ward. She'd passed the Bar, too – did you know? Of course, you must know—' (I didn't, but it felt like bullshit anyway) '—and she was extraordinarily talented in all sorts. Music, chess, all those clever things. And so elegant. Yet she became a *gardener*, of all things. Digging around in the dirt! Though, ha, I suppose we all do that in our own ways. But she gave up all that intellectual status for her plants and her gardens. Naturally she was brilliant at those, too, but really. After you've gone, all people remember is some fields full of weeds. What kind of legacy is that?'

'There was the poetry, too,' I replied, getting a bit defensive, if I'm honest. Who was this woman to be getting snooty about my gran? 'Even though we don't have them all, the actual book. The bits I've seen are properly beautiful. They're like glimpses—' (I was stretching now to find the right words, to do my grandma proud in the face of this hoity woman) '—glimpses of a heart full of love and adventure and passion.'

'"Glimpses of a heart". Hmm,' said Maria, and she left the kitchen for a moment, then came back with a leatherbound book in her hand and held it out to me.

'What's...?' I said, my brain half a second behind, and then I was suddenly raging that she'd hijacked our encounter. 'Don't tell me this is her book.'

'I wish,' she said. 'It's an unauthorised biography. It was given to little old me, I can't tell you by whom. Never officially published, but that doesn't make it any less explosive. The evidence is all in there, it's painstaking. Her real legacy. It's quite clear that Julia Ward wasn't just a grower of mazes, nor an amateur poet mooning over lost loves and what-have-you, like everyone thought. She was extremely deep in the underworld, oh yes, all kinds of terrible activities you

118

wouldn't believe. And no one realised that her writing and her mazes were tied up together, both of them a form of record and communication about what she had been doing all her life. Her poem 'Dusk on a May Evening' involves a long metaphor about a woman with 'two faces'. That little biography shows how she was talking about something else entirely.

'Your family has been talking all this time about dear old Julia like she was some wholesome gardener who wrote a few verses. The lost book of poems may or may not exist, may never have existed, who knows. But this book, this book and a few other documents that I can show you... They give us a solution, perhaps, to the terrible tedious old problem of only having one life to live.'

Maria Ripples-Kismet got up. The spell was broken. I shifted and shuffled on the kitchen stool, and felt the edge of that USB stick in my pocket. Maria climbed on a wooden step and reached up to the highest shelf in one of the cupboards, then brought down an ancient-looking manila folder, half an inch thick with whatever was inside. Marked on the front by hand, in a thick black pen, were the initials *JW*. I flipped it open and saw at the front a set of photographs, blown up, desaturated prints from the 1960s, showing a woman in a minidress and gardening gloves. Her resemblance to me, her face, her whole body, the way she stood, stopped my breath. On the back of one of the photos was written: 'I leave to various future times, but not to all, my garden of consequential choices.'

I handed back the folder of photographs, although I wanted to hold on to it, go through those pictures over and over, eat up the details of my gran's life.

119

Maria went on: 'before I saw those photographs, and that note from your grandmother, I kept asking myself how a story could be infinite. I imagined it as a circle, round and round, and perhaps each time was different because we change, we become different to how we were before. Do you see what I mean?'

I kind of did, barely, so I nodded.

'We are doomed to repeat, that's accurate enough – the sins of our fathers, you know, unlearned lessons from history. And believe me, they are all unlearned. The truth is heavier and richer. The world is more spiteful and delightful than one supposes, dear Amber.

'Anyway, I do enjoy chewing over that kind of thing at a theoretical level, but I was still so perplexed by Julia Ward and this legacy of hers that didn't seem to make sense. And then just when I thought I was at a dead end, that wonderful little book turned up in the post.

'Naturally, my attention was caught by the sentence, "I leave to various future times, but not to all, my garden of consequential choices." That's when I started to get a grip on it. When she says, "to various future times, but not to all," she's telling us that there's more than one future, that just as we have different places all at the same instant, we have different times all at the same instant too.' (I began to think about ketamine, and balloons.) 'We are faced with options, and we try to do the nice thing. All the nasty things drop by the wayside. Except, dear Amber—' (how did she know my name?) '—except they do not. And who is to say what is nice and what's nasty?' Now she was glowing. 'We try to be nice, but why? Who for? Julia rejected binaries! She chose everything, and when you read her poetry, when you walk through her garden, when you read about her life, you see how it worked.'

YES. Hadn't I always known? I was silent, scrambling to piece all the implications together.

'Let's think about... Ms X. She gets an anonymous message on her social media – something abusive, perhaps an unsavoury picture. Ms X will react in some way. Naturally there are various possible outcomes. She can reply sarcastically and block; she can report the sender; they can get into a row; they could even end up getting to know each other and becoming friends. In Julia's work, all the possibilities occur, each one being the point of departure for other possibilities. Sometimes these possibilities meet or cross over. For example, you have come to my house; you're sitting in my kitchen; but your motivations for doing so are infinitely multiple, and actually, my dear, neither one of us knows which future, out of the possible futures spun out of the past, we have arrived at.

'If you're happy to listen to me for a few minutes more, I'd love to read you a couple of passages from dear Julia's work that I've been enjoying recently.'

Maria opened the manila folder and wiggled out a tattered pamphlet. Her face, under the clean kitchen lights, hadn't changed, but I suddenly saw in it a kind of settled authority.

Like a schoolteacher recounting a fable, she read two versions of the same story. In the first, a wife and her husband are each unfaithful. She fucks their gardener in the kitchen when he comes in for a glass of water; he fucks his weightlifting instructor. Neither one ever breathes a word, and they go on to live a long and harmonious life together. In the second, a wife and her husband are each unfaithful. She fucks their gardener in the kitchen when he comes in for a glass of water; he fucks his weightlifting instructor. After some rigorous discussions, the wife and her husband invite the gardener and the weight-lifting instructor to spend a night with them in a hotel room. It is exciting and authentically mind-expanding, but also not so straightforwardly great that they ever do it again, and they go on to live a long and harmonious life together. The husband continues to lift weights, and their garden remains well kept.

I had enough respect for Ripples-Kismet to pay proper attention to all this, although I didn't really care what she was saying so much as the fact I was hearing a proper chunk of Julia's words for the first time, and that, electrifyingly, we were connecting across time and space *right now,* the inside of her head opening up to me in this journalist's plain-but-posh kitchen in deepest West Sussex. So I remember the words at the end of both versions, repeated like some kind of message direct from my grandmother: 'So, in the end, there was no need for any angst at all. There was pleasure, and then there was peace.'

I started to feel something running around my nervous system that I'd never felt before. A sense of the universe and all its possibilities moving through me like a network of sweetly flowing rivers and streams. It was unnerving, I won't lie, but it felt good, too. Quietly exciting. Meanwhile, Maria kept talking:

'Now I don't think Julia was writing some kind of throwaway erotica. All those years she spent on her book? She wasn't wasting her time. She was no doubt aware that her work was likely to be dismissed as flimsy or feminine or, worse, "romance". She knew her talents went way beyond any level she'd ever be recognised for, and I think she decided to turn that to her advantage. Everything we know about her suggests she'd revel in a little mischief, and misdirection. You might even say we can't take anything she writes at face value. And if we consider this underlayer of her work to be the more interesting one, it looks as if she is actually wrestling with a single, perhaps unexpected, theme: *time*. She never looks at it directly, though; in fact she refuses to use the word itself. Why do you think that is?'

I knew the answer but I didn't want to say it straight away. Maria got impatient, and said: 'if you're playing a parlour game, and the answer is umbrella, what's the one word you cannot say?'

'Umbrella,' I said. 'Ella, Ella, Ella.' And I pictured my Ella here, with me, in this kitchen.

'Right,' said Maria. 'When you look at all your grand-mother's work together, including the gardens, her writing, her activities *sub rosa* – everything – you discover she was creating a giant puzzle, on the subject of time. If she had ever used the word, it would have ruined the game. It's obvious once you realise that the absence of the word is the arrow pointing to it. She certainly had some fun with it – at our expense, I might say. You have no idea of the work I've put into trying to understand what she was up to, and, once I had begun to suspect her game, trying to catch her out. But she's always one step ahead. She gets so close, but she never actually lays her cards on the table.

'Once you've seen it, it's so obvious. Her garden of consequential choices is a gift, really, in which she suggests to us a new way of being in the world. Julia did not think of time as uniform or linear. She rejects the idea of death as some kind of mundane ending, a simple, numbing thud that shuts off a life, the end. She believed in an uncountable series of times – like possibilities, but they all happen!' She was getting breathless now, pink in her cheeks. 'We are alive within infinite diverging, converging and parallel times. Like a millefeuille or an endless mountain range or a mycorrhizal network. And we exist in all of them, we all do, everyone who ever was and for all I know everyone who ever will be. This web of time – the strands of which approach one another, bifurcate, intersect or ignore each other through the millennia – embraces *every* possibility. The crucial thing is that there is no good or bad, no right or wrong. No trying to be moral in the hope we might be spared death. You just *are*. I just *am*. And we *do*. Over and over again, all at the same time. In this one, you have come to my house and we discuss your wonderful grandma. In another, you arrived and found me prostrate in the garden. In yet another, I'm throwing a party and you join us but I forget to tell you about Julia. Can you imagine!'

'Wow,' I said. I couldn't help it. Something was taking me over. 'I had you down as a bit of a hack—' (unfair, that; it was the old me getting one final gasp before I went under) '—but you're actually... really into this, aren't you?'

'That's the truth of it as we stand here now,' she said, smiling. 'But remember, in plenty of other layers of reality, I'm just a shallow gossip-monger for the tabloids, selling souls for money, and nothing else.'

The last wave broke over me, and then I, or someone like me, surfaced with an urgency, a call to action. It seemed quite clear that the room we were in and the soft shivering garden beyond were filled with invisible people. Me and Maria Ripples-Kismet, over and over again, looming, clustered and each one busy with her own horrible plan. I stood up, fast, and that vision was gone. I just saw one figure, a man, climbing over that garden gate. It was that rat, that simpering toad, that foul little turd John Morrey.

'I like reality better when I don't think too much about it,' I replied. 'I'm not clever like you, you know? I just find: action speaks louder. Will you show me that file again?'

Maria leaned forward and smiled. It was a smile that dripped with fondness, a smile that revealed the delight she felt as a result of this exquisite, peculiar situation. 'John is here,' she said, and I heard the door handle click, the door opening behind me.

Morrey burst in and then time became soft, juicier, colours bursting out everywhere. A shuddering, shimmering tableau: Maria leaning over me, all creamy-pleased with herself; Morrey's hand reaching out; my body moving at infinitesimal increments, impossibly toward both of them at once. Then a clarity, an exchange between me and Maria, a moment where the world fitted back together. A shift of allegiance.

I won't go into the sticky details of what we did to John Morrey that night in the backyard. It had to be done – and at least one of us enjoyed it. And now he is back out among them, the other scrotes, doing our bidding. One by one, he will bring each of them to their fate.

Don't ask me which side I was on: 'right', ha, or 'wrong', those labels are pathetic and childish and I gave up on them years ago.

My life from now on will, perhaps, be a quiet and unassuming situation, and I suppose I shall never see my dearheart again. She knows, though. The luxury annexe in Maria's garden suits me perfectly. We spend a lot of time together in the beautiful garden, of course (roses, hornbeam, aubergines). We work on our projects, sometimes together and sometimes apart. Maria is teaching me jiu-jitsu. No one knows, and why would they care, about the neverending joy and deep satisfaction of our lives.

# The Grief Hour

## Leila Aboulela & Lucy Durneen

It is just as Linn warned them: it's hard to sleep when it is snowing. Ester's wakefulness has started to feel child-like, regressive, but as if regressing to something new, even if it is still too soon to be able to say what the newness will become. She leaves the blinds open and watches the snow fall into the blank spaces of the forest. It is not true that snow falling is silent. At night they all hear it humming, hollow snowsound skimming along the walls of the research station like there are wings inside the cavities. Their bodies feel the hum and, for a few hours each night, ache in their too-tight skins.

There are rules here, mostly about the communal fridge, and not lighting candles inside the bedrooms, but also about the birch forest behind the research station. The rules say nothing is to be painted or carved onto the trees. The wood pile under the tarp is not to be touched. Outside, Ester notes granite rock formations and starry clusters of yarrow blinking at the frames of the basement windows. Further down the road there is a lake, fringed by darker, heavier pines, with two plastic chairs incongruously arranged on a jetty that pushes out in a dark triangle through bulrushes and ice. The water underneath the ice seems anxious as though it gulps for air. Every now and then, there comes a sound from the depths like someone moving heavy machinery.

At the station they unpack equipment and choose desks in the communal workspace, a white-walled room lined with ceiling-height picture windows that face the pine forest out front. Ester waits to see if anyone is going to take the window with the clearest view of the lake and, when no-one does, sets out her notebooks and a water bottle on the MDF trestle nearest, a staking of some kind of impotent claim that feels vital anyway. She wonders where Tomas might choose to sit, when he arrives. He hasn't replied to her last message, so she doesn't even know when that will be.

'Pine energy is masculine. Birch is feminine,' Ida says, seeing Ester at the window, and Ester smiles and nods, because the birches are leaning knowingly into the wind, as if they are telling her it is not that simple, or not that complicated; everything becomes blurred by the snow in the end.

There is a skull on the back porch, from a dog, maybe, or a goat. The skull is now art, because someone has rested it against a broom in an artful way. The nights are purple and open-mouthed, and the stars wait at the treeline like teeth. The sky moves slowly above. *Sometimes the moon—* Ester writes three words in her journal and then suddenly there is nothing else to say. It is just a complete sentence. Sometimes the moon. But sometimes not the moon, she realises, on

130

the days where the darkness arrives soon after lunch, fully formed, like a lucid dream.

The moon is only for her private journal. In the field journal, which is the one she will upload to her university department, Ester makes notes about geophysical features and inputs data recording mineralogical biomarkers. She explores the labs in the wooden house adjacent to the living quarters. The limited daylight at this time of year will give her some idea, she hopes, of the phototropic capabilities of the plants that might potentially accompany a team on a manned mission to the dwarf planet Ceres, which is one of the settlement destinations they are here to consider for viability. She lies on her bed and turns her face to the pale light of the window, like a tree. Then she texts Tomas.

*Why weren't you on the train?*

The snow falls and Ester cannot sleep. At 2am she is woken by a thought of how, at night, the heart can pause for up to fifteen seconds before beating again. She lies there without moving, wondering if she is still alive inside the hollow space between the *in* beat and the *out*. A silence. Eventually, eventually a beat.

Ester's mother has taught her that in Chinese medicine, 2am is the hour of grief. If you are awake at this time, it is because a part of your body is longing for something that is too far away for it to attain. The bedroom ceiling is smooth and shadowless, and the wings keep humming in the walls, calling her somewhere, outside maybe, or perhaps just deeper into herself. The call from outside is the strongest. Sometimes the longing makes Ester leave her room to sit in the empty kitchen, where she can feel the eyes of tall dark creatures watching her from the other side of the snow. The shadow of the forest makes her think about the thing Tomas said when they first met, how whenever he looked at her everything suddenly became very light. Something inside her tells Ester not to look out of the windows. On those nights, she makes tea, staring hard at the boiling kettle, holding tight to the steaming mug as she walks, head down, through the long corridor back to her room, and the individual cells of her body return to their mourning until the dawn makes its bright entry, like a tired bird, landing.

'Why do you have to go all the way up there?' her mother asked on the drive to the airport, her voice shifting on *there*, as if even the word had become faraway from the rest of the world, and Ester knew she was thinking of the war on the news, the border fence being built against the Russians, the reports of strange balloons in the skies.

Ester had already tried to explain the project more than once. *Think of it like a humanitarian safety net*, was how she put it to her mother, using the language of the grant applications. *Maybe there is a Planet B after all!* NASA began it in the 70s, but spaceflight had advanced so much it made sense to reassess the parameters. 'And in geophysical terms,' Ester had taken care to point out, 'the environment in the region of the Arctic Circle isn't so different from a celestial body. A *planet*—'

Her mother said nothing. In all her attempts to understand Ester's work, it was clear she had never quite grasped that the Earth could be as unknowable as Mars. It was early enough that the sky was still, in some way, a remnant of the day before, and they skimmed along wide and empty roads without saying anything else to each other at all.

*Is this why I came home then?* Ester thought. *To leave again.* To be silently transported to the airport in the blue hour, the moon hyperbolic above the lakes that were not really lakes but excavated gravel pits. Soon after they joined the highway, a live version of an old song had come on the radio, one she used to listen to back in high school, and for a minute she wanted to stop the car and ask someone – although of course there was no-one out there on the road – what year it was. *Baby you're my light*, murmured the singer, once a heartthrob she'd pinned to her bedroom wall. The melody's rising arpeggio seemed to make the car speed up, and the moon flipped through the swiftly moving landscape like a thumb across the pages of a leporello. Ester touched the dark window pane with her cheek, closed her eyes, felt the moon like a savage pull at the water of her body. *Strange, improbable rock up in the sky, you are indeed my light.*

That was two weeks ago and now *there* has become *here*. This lake is a genuine lake, an ancient glacier lake. The moon hovers over it, sometimes low, and at other times so distant that it looks like it might topple from its height and fall out of the world entirely. This is the real blue hour, Ester realises. Not metaphorically blue. Blue like there is really just too much of everything.

~

It had been easy picking him up from the station. All I did was stand with a placard and the name of the research station. People are so trusting. Especially the entitled ones, those who haven't been pushed out of their homes or had their place taken away from them. Safety from harm, like food and warmth, were all people like him had ever experienced. So why should he be wary of anything else? At the station, he just tagged along; accepted the lie that the car was parked further away. He followed me with his head down over his phone.

I held it now and scrolled through his messages. Ester. Ester. 'She'll need to find herself another man,' I said. He was not provoked. Well-trained probably. CIA, Special Service, masquerading as a poet. Nothing fanciful about him.

Which meant also he could see me for what I was. An amateur, yes, but driven... too many people have taken what I once had. I have starved. Left with nothing. Rags, crumbs, bits of papers. Yet here is money for extra-terrestrial travel. The designing of space habitats, blah blah.

He explained, in a tired, patient voice, how space exploration would resolve the world's problems. I remember thinking: he believes this bullshit. Without irony he uses the word 'colonise', exploiting other planets, sucking new places dry, enslaving their inhabitants.

No, he said, there are only humans on Earth.

'How do you know?'

He smirked.

'You're no poet,' I said. 'A real poet would understand humanity.'

For the first time I saw pain in his eyes, and I was satisfied. But I shouldn't have been, I should have wanted more. That was what made me different, how little I need food, clothes, warmth – it's my own way of taking revenge: I take what I need and no more.

I've stopped missing them, stopped chanting their names in the moonlight... Zayn, Sinead, Omar, Gertrude. Shannon and her baby. Keija and Ben, the couple. Mustafa who prayed and died and, after we sent him away to die, we said, we kept saying, things were never the same afterwards. Then began the bickering and the falling out. We took sides, broke up, drifted away. Leaving me bereft. So I trained myself to do without them. I found here, instead, a place. Found I could live by myself, without the cries of the baby, the tears, my tears.

I was content, living far away from the race. I found myself able to hear the hum of the plants, feel the vibrations from the rocks, the moon moving the blood in my veins. I could stand still for hours, looking out at the lake, willing my body to be still and grounded, like a tree.

And then it all fell apart, my peace undone, those two chairs on the cliff edge.

Two plastic chairs at angles to each other, as though two would come and sit in perfect companionship, own the spot, enjoy the view. Was it careless? No, deliberate, a marking of territory, a claim, their entitlement to be here. The chairs were ugly, like spiders, mired in dread that someone would sit on them, that – anytime now – they would come back, at their whim, without any earning of privilege or permission, just resting here.

A declaration of war.

This was in those last days of summer, when the birds flew beneath the cliff I stood on. In my initiation trials I had to watch a flock of sheep fall from those cliffs. Do nothing but accept and let them go, while they, blind in their togetherness, kept running. Afterwards, looking down, I saw their remains, blotches of blood, some of them bleating still. I was to do nothing. Helplessness, too, was part of the lesson. There was no way to tame Nature – the only glory came through letting it make you wilder.

So, before they came to clear the sheep away, I was down on the beach. Helping myself. A sheepskin coat, a rug, the almost-foreign taste of grilled meat. I dreamt that night I was falling, that I was being rolled over, herded, taken away, all jumble and noise and acceleration, a distant knowledge of land rushing up at you.

I failed, of course. As the sheep went over the edge, I had run to save them, screaming out warnings, my voice nothing in the wind. By the time I reached them they were all gone. Even the one last one, the straggler, smaller, not even part of the group, scampering along... he simply followed them all down.

~

The kitchen is, for now, where they assemble to debrief the day. They are still acclimating, so the talk is mostly about themselves and not the work they are here to do, which at this nascent point seems something more like an idea written after a dream and not something anyone is actually paid to do.

Linn is the psychologist. Ida is a digital architect. Martin and Ester are both planetary scientists, although as an astro-palaeontologist, Ester's specialism is very niche, which means somehow Martin has assumed seniority. *Because I work with petroleum!* he says, as if he is worried she'll think it's because he is a man. Sometimes it feels hard to know if her contribution to the team is an asset or a secret tangent to it. The worlds Ester researches may have existed even before what people call the dawn of time – or may not have existed at all – and her work is somewhere in the space

137

between the two. When she first invited Tomas to apply to the International Settlement Project, he had asked, without irony, what her research – so focused on an improbable past – could have to say about the space habitats of the future. 'There's every chance that the environments might prove to have more in common with prehistoric Earth,' Ester told him, but the sentence had sounded wrong, in the way that factually correct sentences in textbooks have no resemblance to the real world. If nothing else, it's becoming increasingly clear to Ester that what she knows about the meaning of life is just dust in a hot, dead wind.

They seek out routines, as if it's inconceivable to just follow the rhythms of the light. There's an intuitive camaraderie that has divided the group by field and seems to draw a clumsy line between theory and practice. The engineers are in an annexe at the far end of the station and have their own kitchenette, which means they are as much of a mystery as the things they do. Ida reports a guilt at preferring Ester's kitchen, with its wide view of the water and better snacks. 'But *engineers*,' she says, and they all nod, in agreement with something that society has never formally articulated but is universally understood. Ida is from Santiago. 'We're a very melancholy people, Chileans,' she says by way of an introduction. 'We're not all just cueca and Bolaño, you know.'

Ester asks if there's a figure down by the water, someone fishing maybe. Linn can't see what Ester can see, a squat cyan shadow blurred against the whiteness of the lake.

'Pretty sure it's just a tree,' Linn says. She pours tea, brings the cup to her mouth, hovers it there without swallowing. There's an archness to it all that makes Ester certain she's being analysed. But later, swiftly turning past the window on the way to the lab, they both see it at the same time, the possibility of limbs, an intent in the posture. Linn wipes down the counter around the teapot more times than is necessary. 'Almost certain it's just a tree,' she says again.

'Almost?'

Wittgenstein's tree, they start to call it. A person from one angle, or something else from another. Martin seems pleased they have an in-joke, as if this is a marker of the group's success. He laughs at their joke and asks Ester if she wants coffee, which she has already figured out is just the start of a ritual, how he warms her up for his questions like you'd roll a lemon in your palms before juicing it. Ester doesn't like coffee, but this isn't her first field expedition – she knows that how you engage with its rituals can assign you to the alpha group. Suddenly it seems important, to be an alpha, to belong to something. Mostly, Ester is not a person who belongs. Scientists cannot even agree on a name for her field.

What Martin wants to know is where the last member of the team is. 'He's cutting it fine,' Martin says. 'Man, this guy!'

'The poet?' Ester says, as if it's the first she's heard of Tomas. She knows what Martin is thinking. She has the same feelings about poets herself sometimes, and Tomas in particular, but there's a code that says scientists aren't supposed to talk about how they feel about poetry. Martin is curious about the delay. He asks questions while he opens and closes cupboards, taking longer to look for things than he needs to, as if the answers are really what's inside.

'Do we even need a poet?' Ida asks.

'We need funding,' Martin says. He pauses with the refrigerator door half-open, letting the space it leaves become a kind of punctuation. 'And the research councils love the A in STEAM.'

'Tomas is just… busy,' Ester says, eventually. 'It's hard to get away from work at this time of year.'

'Too important for us?'

'That's not what I meant.'


But it is exactly what Ester means, in a way. She has known Tomas a long time. He works the same way that he loves people, in flashes, and only sometimes, but she isn't going to tell Martin that. The fact he is, genuinely, brilliant only makes the flashes harsher, like walking into a bright room with a headache. Thinking of him, and where he might be, feels like a stone is dropping down through her solar plexus, and Ester wants to be alone someplace she can turn the stone over and over until the feeling has gone, but the coffee maker uses real beans, which means Ester has to wait in the kitchen longer than she planned, until Martin has ground the coffee she doesn't want. She pretends to inspect the contents of her assigned cupboard. When he depresses the grinder he gestures in a way that could indicate a small irritation or be a

140

mime for the inexorable march of time. *Sorry!* they both say, when they accidentally open the same drawer, reaching for a spatula she knows neither of them intends to use.

Days pass. They walk to the lake, they return from the lake. They take samples, file data. Sometimes they sit on the plastic chairs on the jetty, watching the changing colours of the ice, until their fingers make crunching sounds when they flex them inside their gloves. Other times they walk as far as the cliffs on the other side of the forest, where there are rumours of petroglyphs decorating the stone. But they don't find the petroglyphs, and the high, angular cliffs make Ester uneasy, reminding her of a picture book her father used to read her, about an ancient spirit people that hid in caves and imitated their parents' voices to lure children into the dark. There are fragments of skulls here too, the same sloping shape as the one beside the back door, but these skulls are not arranged carefully into art. They are scattered, as if something has been gutted and then scavenged by the frozen air.

Returning to the station late one night, Ester finds a pot of yarrow tea on the kitchen table, with a note inviting its finder to pour a cup. The tea is pale gold, and leaves float in it like stars. When Ester takes off the lid, wary, there is a bitter smell, but the molten sky is clear inside the pot, and she can see all the way to its bottom, down and down, where one by one, eventually the petal stars go out, and she is just alone again in the kitchen, in the dark.

~

I hold the cliffs in awe. To stand and watch the birds fly beneath me, that is the privilege. Humanity is knowing not to take the fatal step. Understanding your place in the world, unlike those sheep, falling, confused, below.

Until: the scientists from the new station. The two chairs. More territory, more space. Chairs like the flags they'll pitch on other planets. Soon there will be laws, entitling them to whole planets, like deeds to land. The way Africa was carved. Granting planets as compensation to those history has fucked. That's us – shooting our quarrels into outer space.

Two of the researchers come and sit back, look up, their sunglasses tinted falsely. They slouch. They eat too – packets of crisps, nuts, protein shakes, leaving their junk behind, traces of themselves that will last forever, poisoning birds and plants. Not enough for them now their station, this warm wheezing building, but also now the fields where our children once ran.

I must put an end to this. If the terrain is unsafe, they will go away.

Tomas listened well – a spy or poet, I don't know – but to him I found I could talk as I had always wanted.

'In the past,' he said, 'they would have called you a hermit. It is strange how many more of you there are now. There's a lot of homelessness, people distrustful of society.'

He spoke about yogis and the threat they'd posed to the colonial authorities. He spoke about their peculiar powers. Able to sleep on a bed of nails, surviving though buried alive.

'Yes!' I said, 'yes! I can sleep standing up. I can stop my mind from dreaming.'

He looked puzzled. 'No, you are a secular yogi,' he said. 'You would not have special powers.'

Even tied up, he still pervaded my home. I watched him sleeping, head lolling, his breath deep and steady. His air, the smell of his body, flakes of skin, hair, spit, blood, spreading out towards me, enveloping me.

I woke him up.

'We want to know,' he would say, 'if, instead of searching for a viable planet, it might be possible to adapt Ceres – how a womb expands for the growing foetus.'

If I killed and buried him, the weight of his body would linger here even more. If I buried him elsewhere, his spirit would surge back. If I herded him away and let him go, he would leave behind an imprint that others would follow. An invasion of bodies and questions.

I had to get away, before I was taken over completely, make yet another new home.

He watched me gather some of my belongings.

'Let me call Ester, before the battery dies.'

I hammered the phone into the wall above his head, then left him and walked out, up the slope covered with snow, to the cliff edge. All was white. Beneath my feet stretched a layer of cloud so thick I could not see the beach. I dropped my things. Put my left foot out. I felt nothing underneath. But, resting on something more than air, I felt, somehow, balanced. I shifted my right foot, moved forward. The edge of the cliff now behind me, the mist parted then and I saw I was standing over the beach, hovering in the wind like those birds soaring below.

~

One evening Martin invites the engineers to play Exquisite Corpse and drink wine in what they are now calling the Theory Kitchen. The joke is supposed to be that only here with the scientists does the real thinking happen, but it turns out the engineers are annoyingly good at writing darkly funny stories. The sky accelerates towards evening, and the mood moves with it into something as smooth and dark as tourmaline. The wine is a heavy Carmenere, chosen by Ida, and makes Ester feel quickly drunk, then sleepy. Martin is advocating for a new research strand on astro-mining. 'If it's possible,' he keeps repeating, '*if it's possible*, the resources on just *one* asteroid would totally fund the whole damn mission.' He keeps jabbing towards the sky outside the window, but Ester cannot tell if this is because there is something invisible and important out in the dark, or if his hands don't know they are moving. She is tired of him always talking about money. One of the engineers lifts his head wearily from the table. 'Do you think,' he asks, 'that we have entered the time just before the disaster?'

'Now you're thinking like a Chilean,' Ida says, and raises her glass.

That night the sound of the wind puts Ester to sleep. Or maybe it is the wine, whirring through her blood. She dreams she is on a rock hurtling through space, brilliant with gold and cobalt. At first it seems she is flying on it, but then there are reins in her hand, and she is guiding it, like a radiant horse, out into the shimmer of distant space. 'You're free now,' she whispers to the rock, and she can feel its gratitude shudder between her legs. She has the sudden feeling that there is someone on the rock beside her, but the feeling changes and instead the presence is inside her, and it is a branch, first one and then many, shooting a cold, green pulse that pushes up along her neck and out through her jugular, and when she wakes up, she is scratching her hand at her throat, reaching for leaves. There is both relief and disappointment to find only her skin. Then Linn, at her door, banging it hard with a fist. 'You're screaming the place down,' she says. 'What the hell, Ester?'

They present their research on a weekly basis, sitting in the studio on flat cushions that slide on the laminate floor and make even the most agile of them somehow graceless. Ester clicks through a PowerPoint and explains that for now she's mostly focusing on ways to stimulate plant growth in a low-nitrogen environment. She hopes the physicists can advise her on the likely gravitational fields of the various celestial bodies of the study. Ceres is mostly clay and ice, for example. 'The real mystery is light,' is how she concludes her third report. 'On Earth, plants grow upward towards it. I'm wondering how we might have to compensate for that.' She is hoping it might sound intriguing, or even game-changing, as if she might save the world with what she knows about plants, but the physicists are distracted by the sliding cushions, and before Ester has shut down her laptop it's Linn's turn.

Linn's presentation is all about the psychology of group dynamics in space, how the initial euphoria of interstellar travel wears off fast. She seems louder than normal, as if the words are buzzing off her skin. 'Think *Lord of the Flies*!' she shouts at them. 'Or that film where students go crazy in a bunker!' Now everyone sits up very straight, imagining, perhaps, the various madnesses they might be susceptible to, 1.74 astronomical units from this, their home planet.

'When it comes to it,' Linn says, surveying their faces sternly, 'You'll all be put to the test out there. Will you step up and lead, or will you lose it? I want you to think about that!'

Linn wants them to think about it right now, in pairs. 'What would your mythical poet have to say?' Martin asks Ester, and she resents the way Tomas has been attached to her, without her noticing, like a burr on a coat. Belonging to

146

him was something she had never quite managed of her own accord. But then it seems even worse that he has become *mythical*. Even when absent, he is able to make her feel like she is slipping away from herself.

'I don't know about you,' she says instead, 'but I'm getting the feeling it might be Linn who goes crazy and kills us all.'

Martin leans forward and moves a strand of hair that has stuck to Ester's eyelashes. 'Tell me about the light,' he says, and Ester thinks: dear god, he is trying to seduce me.

Maybe, she thinks later, *slipping* is not quite the right way to put it. It is a less consensual sensation, as if something is being peeled away from her, like she is now the birch tree and all her bark is being stripped away.

Ester spends more and more time at the lake. She sits in the plastic chair, which is covered with a filmy layer of ice, and stares at its empty counterpart. The thing about this-time-just-before-the-disaster is that everything looks so entirely normal. The lake still murmurs and groans. Around the chairs there are trails of ice on the jetty, like they have been skating around when no-one was looking. It has been more than two months since she heard anything from Tomas, and she isn't sure if she is less concerned for his well-being than humiliated by his absence. 'Where are you?' she asks, out loud. 'Where *are* you?'

'Who are you talking to?'

Ester hasn't seen Ida walking across the field and now she is embarrassed. She is relieved that it isn't Linn who's found her this way, and might see it as another opportunity

147

to assess her mental competence. Ester doesn't want to go into space anyway, if that's where the catastrophe is taking them, but the possibility of space travel suddenly seems beside the point.

'You were waving your arms around,' Ida says. 'Want some company?'

Ester shakes her head, no, although it comes out as a gasping noise full of such surprising words it makes Ida sit down in the other chair. 'Damn, it's cold,' she says, as if she was expecting something else.

'Do you feel guilty?' Ester asks.

'About?'

What Ester wants to say is *everything* but, because she is saying it here, by this lake at sundown, the moment would be a cliché. She can't let it be the kind of moment you'd see in a film, the epiphany, the bright and sudden coalescing of it all. But it's taking too long for her to choose a different way to answer, and she can see Ida is expectant now. 'What we're doing,' Ester says eventually. 'Do you think it's right?'

'Why wouldn't it be right?'

'Maybe humanity's supposed to just bow out gracefully. Maybe resettlement isn't the answer, and it's just… time.'

Ida shrugs. 'Life has always been moving from one place to another. Everything is transient. Everything wants to change. Even bacteria can transfer from one astronomical body to another. Who knows where we originated at all.'

'Don't say it,' Ester says. '*We're all stardust*. Just don't.'

'All of this is just a theory,' Ida says. 'Don't sweat it.' She breathes into her hands and claps them hard together, like a conclusion. 'Anyway, I thought you meant the poet. I thought you were going to say you and Martin had buried him out in the woods.'

Ester rolls her eyes, but the stone in her belly drops sharply, and for a moment she wonders. 'I don't think Tomas is coming,' she says instead, and something feels impossibly final about the words, like she already knows that no-one is ever going to ask her about Tomas again. For a moment, Ida's face relaxes, then snaps back to attention. She points to the horizon, to a cluster of stars dreaming into view; 'Hey look – Venus!' and although she doesn't want to, Ester can do nothing but follow her gaze upwards.

The longer they sit by the lake, the less the lake looks like a place on Earth. All of the shapes and shadows look faintly recognisable, but as if someone has moved them just out of place. Ester catches sight of Wittgenstein's tree. A silhouette faint behind it. The imprint of a person against the white, white sky.

'It's a *tree*,' Ida says, softly. Her hand touches Ester's arm, but it seems to have fallen out of alignment with the world. As if someone was describing the feeling of a person's hand resting on your arm – the weight of it, the soft squeezing – and Ester is trying very hard to imagine what that would be like. From one body to another, something transferred.

~

149

How have I lived so long? It feels like another lifetime but, somehow, though the sunlight is painful, I am still breathing, still sitting over the cliffs. I leave the cave only at twilight, at the balance of dark and light, the moment that beginning meets end. Once, in the odd tilted stillness before a storm, I opened my mouth to exclaim but found my tongue heavy, the words if not my own: the strangest sense, the sound of one's own voice.

And then, eventually, they claimed this too. Explosions, earthquakes, showers of land collapsing around their relentless burrowing.

Upside down mouths, out of the cave on a stretcher. A rock hurtling through blackness. No space anywhere. Pressed up against a diminishing future.

I was stifled by chemical smells, the pain of people's proximity. Examined, poked, extracted. Under lights, everyone's face a shock.

Pictures of the hunchback found hiding in a cave. Shrivelled, wild, head back, sniffing the air like a rodent. A murderer now also. But I didn't kill him – I kept him safe. Her messages to him became fewer, and then, eventually, stopped. Good. Maybe she would understand it all by herself, without his glorifying it. The bard of an invading force, paid in whatever he would find in their rubble.

When I asked him to read aloud her messages he would just cry. This, he said looking round the cave, this might be the best thing to happen to her.

Everything is squeezed here. The nursing home is surrounded by high walls. Tranquilisers for the screaming. Heavy food, clockwork, pills and capsules, teeth replaced. I repeat the nurses' words senselessly: 'you can still be of use,' 'I can still be of use.' In the yard, alone, at twilight again, I begin to get my bearings. In the stillness, as if among the snowy trees again, I resume my old work with patience although, with everything new in me, I am not sure if I can still fly.

There is a big screen in the dining area. The New Space, it declaims, the Natural Resettlement, where there's always room to flourish. What familiar poetics...

Maybe there *can* be space for everyone, but there is nowhere I want to be anymore.

Kwasi can no longer walk – he and I have made up a game with chess pieces, become absorbed in it, taking pleasure in the shape of the pieces in the hand.

Kwasi says, 'we don't have to do anything. Just be. Breathing, dying or already dead, we will be of use up there. Ter-rah-form-ing. Making Earth out of us. Germs, dry flesh, old bones – our dreams and voices making the air sweeter. Even prisoners, refugees, useful now.'

Kwasi won our game, but he and some others vanished the next day.

A week later, waking in the van, its door slid open. On the airfield, a ship the size of a city. Hundreds boarding, hundreds, and they, we, us, the wretched of the earth, gasping, tottering, or wheeled, sedated, bewildered; even children, tumbling in cages, chubby fingers, mouths open.

I plant my feet into the ground, strong at last, ready to fly.

Stretcher or wheelchair? Surrounding me. Stretcher or wheelchair? I let go of my stick, hands out to fly, but, then, stop. For where is there to go?

~

The snow wakes Ester in the grief hour. Her eyes swim to meet the dark. The humming in the walls surrounds her, then seems to move from the walls right into her body. The hum tells her to get out of bed, and follow it to the door that leads to the porch. It gets louder, except it is not actually a noise. For a moment Ester holds her breath, considering if it might just be the sound of her whole heart trembling. Her body waits without her telling it to. But then it is inside her legs, her belly, a sharp and vivid feeling like a current sparking through her blood. The source of the current seems far away on the other side of the porch door. Something recedes in her. Then it returns, larger than before.

Ester heads across the porch, past the sheep's skull and the shadow of the broom, out through the quiet forest, towards the silhouette of the tree that might be a person. The tree stands, resolutely a tree, looking out over the water, and the hum propels her forward until she is leaning against its trunk. Into her cheek it whispers something. She remembers attending a conference once in a national park, girdled by mountains, remembers a local girl who spoke to her; told her to be a good relative to the land. 'We have to act a thing before we can be

152

it,' she had said. Ester had wondered how the girl, so young, knew so much about things that Ester had made her whole life about studying. But this girl just knew the things, the way you know how to walk, or digest food. It made the studying seem small, or blind, as if all you had to do to understand was go outside into the mountains and breathe.

The sounds of the forest tell Ester to lie down on the snow. She hears the roots of the trees deep in the ground. The outbreath of branches above her. She holds herself still. How long would the transformation take, to become the tree? She waits. The last of the light disappears into the lake and snaps into darkness like a door closing.

Somewhere a howl from a distant dog. A whole night of moon. The sky unmade with light. Deer track heart-shaped prints across the bright wide fields, and the stars looking on.

# Apricots

## Tim MacGabhann & Ben Pester

I'm fucking dictating this. Any mistakes are because of the computer. It took a while to get this all set up. I had to learn about it all. You'll get the jist anyway. It starts now, right:

Hello B███. You'll never guess who came to see me! Steven Bucket, that's who. He was here at my place. And he says he saw you.

It wasn't the main reason for his visit, he was supposed to be there about something else, but he dropped it into the conversation so many times it was obvious he wanted to talk about you. Remember when we were younger and he would always need to have a piss just before we went to work? Hopping around. It was like that. Embarrassing. So, anyway, I ask him – oh right, you saw that prick did you?

Yeah, he tells me, and then he's forgotten everything else and it's all about the amazing adventure he had when he saw you unexpectedly, in the middle of the day. As you can imagine, I was rapt.

It was in May, he said. A bright morning in May, and Stevie was out looking for his ingredients. He told me it was a Saturday. He said it all carefully, and every few words he'd look at me, expecting me to admit that, yes, I knew you were coming in May, but of course I had no idea. I don't keep an eye out for you. I'm not really connected anymore. Everything has changed. But after Stevie was here, I did make some enquiries, and I know for a fact you aren't here anymore. I have your current address, obviously, or how did I fucking send you this? But there's no trace of you at all in England now. I found out the hotel you stayed – it looked like the kind of place you'd choose, from the website. I only glanced, but I imagine you stayed in the Sinatra suite. I can see you in there, sleazing the place up. Fucksake it really cuts me up even thinking about you coming here. Thinking of you on a bed! Jesus fucking christ.

Anyway, Stevie[1] saw you in a shop, he said, which as he spoke turned out to be not a shop but a noodle place. His grasp of important versus useless details has not improved at all.

Stevie goes there to buy dried fish, as I'm sure you must have noticed since he buys it by the ten kilo pack. He says a doctor – some prick on the web I expect – told him that dried fish is going to prolong his life, so now he eats nothing but dried fish in broth. You were in the noodle place where he goes to buy it.

---

1 Steven has a slim, long tail. His briefcase is of crocodile leather and is coloured somewhere between cherry red and deep black.

He said that you didn't see him, but I couldn't tell if he was lying. Or maybe he was just not sure, or he could have been refluxing – he has this fucking reflux he does now, it's rank. He back pukes. A bit of bile slishes up and he burps and swallows it back. He's doing this about once every ten minutes. I almost made him stand in a corner but, if I'm honest, I think he would've done it, and it would have depressed me.

So, I wonder, did you see him? You must have seen him. That's what you do, you see people. You go to places and look at things. You suck in everything the light touches and process it. So you saw him, and I like to think you considered just leaving it all alone. The man's buying dried fish by the armful, he's obviously not well. He's ferreting around. Maybe I shouldn't drag him into this. That's what you would have thought. Stevie the fucking Bucket. So I assume you didn't feel like you had a choice but to let him see you so he would tell me. I don't know why. I don't understand any of this, and I don't fucking like it. I was alright not seeing Stevie and I was more than fucking alright not hearing from you! But here we are. Here we fucking are.

Stevie could not tell me how you were. He couldn't say how you were faring, from the way you looked.

Not ill, he said. Definitely not ill.

On his mind, I think, the illness. You'll have noticed his clothes are a little bit empty. His chin's gone completely.

Only thing he mentioned, you were wearing a sweater that 'looked ok' and your coat was new. Not that long green spectacle you used to go around in. He described you eating noodles. Effortless, he said, clean.

Anyway. He came and told me – what he said was 'straight away' but actually it had been three days. He saw you on Monday, and then he came to see me about it on Thursday. There's some news for you, from our little English town. The news is, you still have to wait for Stevie the Bucket. Doesn't matter who you are, or how important it is, you have to let him go through his processes. In his flat for a whole day just trying to get together a broth. Another day nosing around. Who knows. Who knows what he does once he's filled himself up with rehydrated donburi or whatever the fuck.

The other reason he came round here to see me was because a letter arrived. You'll see that soon, the letter. It obviously isn't this fucking letter. It's more of a package really, the other thing. You'll see – I actually like the idea of you holding that other package and wondering what the fuck to do next!

He looked like he'd been baked alive – Stevie, I said, what's happened to you? But you know, the Bucket, he doesn't speak. Just comes into the house, no hello, barges in like a hungry little kid who's seen the biscuits on a table behind you. Except there's no biscuits – his diet, right? So instead there's just space, he wants to eat up the space in my living room. He's walking in circles.[2] Sit down, Stevie, I say.

2 His mother walked in this way too, around rooms, in his house, in the school dinner hall where she worked lunchtimes. She walked in this ponderous way and smiled only at us, Stevie's mates, who looked out for him, as she saw it. Her tail was of gold threads and her briefcase was classic black leather that shone like oil. She would tell us the names of the clouds, she knew them all.

For christs sake sit down. He does not sit down. He's got a letter for me.

Fine, give me the letter, I say.

He doesn't hear me. He just keeps ambling around the living room. He's saying it's hot outside, he's worn the wrong clothes. He asks for some water, and I go and get it like I'm his maid. Does he drink this water? No he doesn't. He puts it loudly on my glass coffee table. I try and tell him about coasters, but what's the point.

He smells awful, by the way. That fish diet has made him smelly and paranoid. I don't see how it's good for his health. The man is going yellow. You know? Jaundice. He probably has something going on that he will never discuss. We're of that age now I suppose. Cancer. Why not? I'm watching him and remembering something someone told me about apricots.

Apparently, learning that he was dying from cancer of the kidneys, a famous tech billionaire[3] commissioned a load of research to try and save his life. Hundreds of millions, he sank into it. Commandeering researchers, university buildings, a hospital wing, I'm told.

The scientists rushed around, did their best attempt at looking busy in order to secure the cash, but even the billionaire must have known it was useless. It takes decades to develop even the slight improvements in cancer care. And you can't just drop whatever project you're in the middle

---

3 The tech billionaire's tail was of green dancing ribbons and his briefcase was brown like his father's.

of doing, so there's no good scientists actually available immediately. So it's all ageing professors and students with wild theories. They have no choice but to come up with experimental stuff, you know? Stuff that is clinically useless, but they have been paid to innovate so they innovate.

They gave him a whole raft of ideas, untested drugs, and theories, but the one the billionaire settled on was dried apricots.

He declared them a miracle food – told everyone they produced an enzyme or whatever that could grind cancer cell division to a halt. He ate a dried apricot every fifteen minutes for the rest of his life.

And do you think it helped? Of course it didn't!

It made no difference whatsoever. If anything, according to the rumour, it killed the billionaire faster. Well that's Stevie and his dried fish. Tragic, you know? He must be sick and keeping it to himself. I hope I'm wrong. I do, but anyway, I'm telling you that he was here, parading round my lounge, and I'm losing my rag with him – he still hasn't given me the letter. I'm happy to admit I was feeling less sympathetic than I should have been.

After a while, he calmed down. I managed to get him to sip a bit of that water. I take a chair on the opposite side of the living room – it's a big room. I like a big room, lots of space, no shit on the walls. Calming. I take a seat on the opposite side of the room and I try to get him to explain to me about the package.

I hear all about his day. I hear all about how he saw you. About your appearance. Your coat. Your hair is still there, just about, apparently. He tells me about you. We talk about you. I'll be honest, I did not enjoy it. I prefer to think of you as gone.

Not dead, but also just no longer with us.

To be honest, if it weren't for this fucking package, I wouldn't even be in touch now. I hear you like noodles? Who gives a shit. I'd have been able to forget about you easily if it was just the noodles. I'm assuming they have noodles out there where you are now. If you have anything further to say to me, you can go through Stevie, but don't expect a reply. Don't expect anything from me again.

~

Alejandro[4] parked his white Camry outside the villa, got out, and ducked under the yellow and black DO NOT CROSS tape. A street vendor[5] had pitched up. A vendor always pitched up wherever more than four people had gathered, whether for breakfast, or for a football match, or for a murder, as was the case here. Alejandro ducked back across the yellow and black DO NOT CROSS tape to see what the vendor had.

He nudged among plastic packets of habas and churritos and peanuts. He picked up the churritos and squinted at

---

4 Alejandro's tail was meaty and contained 18 additional vertebrae. He was in and out of physiotherapy as a kid. His briefcase had stickers from cereal boxes all over the surface concealing entirely whatever was underneath.

5 The Vendor's tail was amputated at birth to prevent blood loss. His briefcase had silver clasps shaped like monkey paws.

them. He'd gone out with a woman the previous year who always ate churritos, always smeared his face with the chilli dust that coated the little fried sticks of corn or imitation corn or whatever it was when it got on her fingers. She had thought it was cute, he supposed. He dropped the churritos back and bought a packet of habas instead. Then he went under the DO NOT CROSS tape and crossed over to the villa.

He wasn't happy about being called out of the city, even though the drive south wasn't bad at this time of day, going against the flow of the traffic – his sleeves rolled up and one arm resting along the open window to catch the cool pulse of the wind on his skin, mist coiling and uncoiling over the fields, a cut of freshness to the air that had yet to be driven off by all the cars chugging north.

As he came to the high gate in front of the villa, a uniform cop[6] from the local force with a big moustache and a bigger paunch gave him a jaunty salute that knocked back the peak of his cap. Alejandro gave him a stare of hard incredulity to fuck with him, then said, 'good morning.'

'All good, detective?'

'You tell me,' Alejandro said, and bobbed his chin at the murder house.

The uniform cop sucked his teeth and said, 'it's these Airbnbs, detective. People walk into any old thing when they think the photos look nice.'

---

6 The cop's tail was standard issue bison swish. His briefcase bore the logo of a long-expired football team.

'Airbnb?'

The uniform cop nodded and fished out his phone.

'See, here,' he said, pinching the screen to zoom in the image. 'Looks all nice on the listing.'

'Bargain for what it is,' Alejandro said.

'Well, think about it, you know. How it is here. All the things happening in the hills and all.'

'Gang stuff, I assume you mean.'

The uniform cop shrugged and said, 'you get far enough out in the sticks and that's all there is. Farms are all empty. Think you can get someone knocked off for about four thousand pesos out here – it's that competitive.'

'Half the city rate,' Alejandro said.

'Yeah, but the quality of the hit?' The police wavered his head from side to side.

'Iffy,' said Alejandro. 'Yes. And the owners. What're they like?'

The uniform cop looked uneasy for a moment and said, 'oh, look, I mean, you only need to see the place. Connected, you know.'

'Connected how?'

The uniform cop said the name of a minister and said, 'his cousin.'

'Oh, Jesus,' said Alejandro, and put the palm of his hand to his forehead. That did it. He popped open the habas.

'I'm sorry, detective.'

'That's alright,' Alejandro said. He held out the packet of habas to the uniform cop, who took a couple. 'Not like you killed him.'

'Or rented him the place, detective.' He cracked a haba between his teeth.

'And what, they live in the place? And rent the room out? Or what?'

The uniform cop munched and nodded and then said, 'bit of a cloud over this cousin. Rumours, you know. Nothing solid.'

'But to the effect that…?'

'To the effect that he lost his job at a school in the city for something with the kids, you know? And so the minister puts him up here where maybe the stink lines don't follow him all the way.'

'So this cousin rents the room out. Our corpse in there could just be someone on holiday who said the wrong thing to their gracious host? And the cousin: where's he? We have a line, don't we?' Alejandro said.

The cop shrugged and ate the second haba and said, 'I don't know. You're the detective.'

'Oh, we've a line. And not very much time.'

Alejandro moved towards the gate and the uniform cop held it open and Alejandro stepped through into the garden of the villa and went up the drive.

The villa was alright, too, boxy, dark blue, the paint job so thick and fresh that one whole side of it threw back a panel of reflected glare. A couple of forensics people[7] sat on the outdoor steps that led up to the top floor, their hoods and

---

7 The forensics people had tails with secret names. Each carried a black suitcase like Stevie's mother.

masks off, passing a pack of chilli-dusted roasted churritos back and forth. He scowled as he walked towards them. Ave de paraíso flowers nodded at him from among stalks of agapanthus all the way up the drive. Beads of dew coated the stems. He let his fingertips trail among them, felt the cool sprink of the drops, felt like, the murder aside, it wasn't going to be such a bad day maybe. The male technician, whom he didn't recognise, gave Alejandro a nod and a straight-line smile; the woman, his friend Teresa[8], turned at his approach and held the packet of churritos out to him.

'Thanks,' he said, and wiggled one out.

'It is fucking horrible up there,' Teresa said. 'Just FYI.'

Alejandro shook a handful of churritos out into his palm, squinting up the steps that went up the side of the house, towards a shed-sized outbuilding whose door was ajar. Dim light and the scraping of plastic bristles spilled through the gap, the shadow of a man's broad back moving back and forth in the gloom. He needed glasses, he knew he did, but who had the time to get these things checked out. He chewed on a churrito, dropped his gaze towards the forensics van parked outside the front door of the villa. The body was in there, bag zipped up. Behind it, through the window, was a timbered room full of box files and leather-bound books.

'In what way horrible?' Alejandro said.

'Almost all of them,' said the male technician. He was young, geeky looking. Alejandro gave him the same look

---

8 Teresa had a double tail in the puma style. At school she made them spin like a cartoon animal. Her briefcase was made of aluminium.

as he'd given the cop by the gate, then handed the pack of churritos back to Teresa.

'I think they made him drink bleach,' Teresa said.

'The smell of fish soup,' the male technician said. 'Really incredible. You get that with someone who drinks bleach?'

'You get jets of black gunk all over the floor with fish soup?' Teresa said back.

'You get all sorts,' the male technician said. 'You get all sorts.'

Alejandro looked back and forth between Teresa and the male technician and then back up the steps. The shadow was on its knees now, scrubbing back and forth, hard. Alejandro looked over at the gleam of the swimming pool, the fat slap of water against tiles, the 7am light dripping glycerine orange from the long tines of the palm trees. He ran the blade of his hand up and down his sternum, breathing in for five seconds and out for five seconds, the way the yoga videos he liked told him to, then took out his bag of habas and popped one into his mouth and slowly crunched.

''Scuse me,' he said, then went up the stairs, still munching the habas.

~

So, here I am. What's left of me after a week in this country. I got off the plane in Mexico City and as soon as that air hit me I realised I shouldn't have come. I gave a taxi driver[9]

---

9 The taxi driver had no tail. His suitcase was a patent white leather with brass clasps and a 9-digit combination lock.

your address. He had the worst cab in the rank, you know? The one with a towelling cover on the steering wheel. Chewing and smoking a long cigarette at the same time. Him.

Can you get me to this address please?

He didn't answer, but started the engine, waited for me to get in. Can you get me there? I repeated. You know the address?

Still no words. But he drove me into the city. Lungfuls of hot petrol air smooshed at me as we flew along the highway. I looked at the other cars, the road signs. The differences that creak against what a road ought to look like. Soon the buildings became older, more ruckled up. He drove me round this enormous park. I've never seen such a beautiful park. The buildings all around it were pink and crumbling like mint cake. I felt like I could take a soft bite out of every facade.

I kept saying, it's beautiful, to myself. And, fucking Mexico! I couldn't believe I was here. It was almost magical, really, despite how lost I was. Despite how alone it felt to be here, to be looking for him when I knew already he would not be there. Every time I thought of seeing you, alive or dead, it was immediately followed by a kind of nausea. But this place is beautiful, I'll say that. I hate it too.

When we got to the address I have been writing to (without a reply – thanks for that, yeah) the polite man on reception told me you were gone.

Where? Where is he gone?

I don't know what you paid the front desk guy[10], but he turned his back on me like I was sunshine in his eye. As though I hadn't ever even existed, he swivelled slowly around on his lumbar-support assisted chair and started pecking with his fingers at the computer. The computer and the chair were in a sort of alcove, built into the wall behind the desk.

When I called to him to turn back around and talk to me, he reached up and pulled a red curtain across. Like a shower curtain almost, but made to look like a theatrical curtain, so now all I could see was the back of his naked ankles jiggling as he snapped his little computer buttons.

A deep voice, very close, was then asking me if it could be of any assistance. It was the security guard.[11] He had left his post at the front door and now he was standing behind me, speaking into my neck, reassuring me that he had got me a taxi to my hotel.

The streets are beautiful in Mexico City. The actual streets themselves. The dust is warm. It feels like you could live outdoors, if it weren't for the violence. Safe but not safe. Stevie must have hated it here. He must have hated dying.

---

10  Front desk guy had weeping sores all over his tail because he never dried it properly after swimming. His briefcase was ultra-thin and had a plastic handle.

11  The security guard had a tail of glittering pompom strands in pink, yellow and black. His briefcase was dark brown leather with concertina edges.

I've had to purchase a shirt – a Hawaiian shirt. I'm in Mexico, which is not Hawaii but I can tell you, I'm in my shirt every day. The sun cleans it.

Muy guapo, that's what the cheeky fucker in the clothes shop said. Muy guapo. Which as you know means I look Very Sexy. A chicken without any skin at all, that's how it makes me look. Shorts as well. It's so hot here. They speak English though, and that's good.

I found the place where he died. Out of the city, I could feel my sweat turning into dust on my skin, and the dust in turn becoming airborne and returning to the churches. The cycle of Christ and polyester. Although it's all Mary down here. Three Marys.[12] I wonder if you were there when he died. I find it hard to believe that you actually did it.


I spent the night in a sort of motel. There's a bedroom, a place to park. The room looks separate, like a fucking motel, but I wake up in the morning and there's an old lady[13] looking at me. She's poking her head in from a door I never knew was there.

Come, she says.

What now?

Breakfast. Coffee.

---

12 The three Marys had tails of pale blue light. Their suitcases were made in Japan in the 1980's.

13 The old lady's tail was just a fake lion's tail from some junk shop. Her suitcase was woven from straw.

Now? Ahora? (I know that ahora means 'now' because I have been saying it fucking repeatedly since I got here. I'd like to go now. I'd like to hire a car, now. I'd like information about any dead Basildon gringos you have here, right ahora please).

It's funny. They know I'm nothing here. I can't be tough. I've got precious few connections. So I'm sort of just English. I could be in Mallorca asking for sausages and beans – you just have to hope it works.

Stevie, it turned out, was in the paper. There's a sort of reporter in the city who seems to enjoy reporting on the death of white Europeans. Especially gangsters who should not even be here.

I didn't realise this until I paid some child[14] about £400 in pesos for information. He more or less read me the paper after leaving me to wait for him in this bar with an interior the colour of boiled beef.

Wait here, he said.

You've got my money, I replied and spread my arms and smiled. Like you know, how you would with a kid. This little boy laughed at me, said something to the huge man at the bar and then went off.

I wiped pale grit off the rim of the bottle and drank my weak beer. It tasted of tin. I watched some of the Liverpool game that was on the TV in the corner of the room, in a cage. I hoped it would relax me but I have never felt so far from

14 The child's tail was tough like an alligator's. His briefcase was mustard-yellow plastic and it banged on his little legs when he walked.

home as I did from the green on that caged television. The boys[15] flowering on the pitch like bleeding tulips. I could touch it, I thought, English grass. But I couldn't. I didn't even have that, the power to reach up and touch the screen of English grass. I was trapped there until the kid got back.

A fly was trapped in there too, that thing buzzed at me incessantly. Flies are hungrier in Mexico, I have noticed. Leaner. Electric. Not like those dobbers we have back home. English flies are slobs. I tried to imagine a fight between our flies and this one. I gave them voices. Fear is a fucker, isn't it? I was doing anything I could to avoid even one second of eye contact with that big bastard at the bar.[16] I could tell he was staring at me, in the peripheral vision, I could feel him staring at me. The airport at Mexico City is built in the shape of a fly, did you know that? An 'A' or a fly. One of those. I haven't researched this, it's just what I saw from the sky.

After what felt like a lifetime, while I lost about a pint of sweat trying to avoid looking towards the bar, the kid finally came back. Like I said, all he had with him was the paper.

Your friend, he might not be so good, he said. By which he meant, Stevie was dead. He helped me with the address of the house where he died. Los Tres Marias, he told me.

---

15 The tails and the briefcases of the Liverpool players were too blurry to make out properly.

16 The big bastard at the bar had a tail of paper streamers. His briefcase was the kind favoured by roadies to carry delicate sound equipment on tour.

171

Into another taxi I went. This time to the car rental place about a mile from the airport. There, I asked the teenager[17] working the desk if he knew of Los Tres Marias.

Sure, he said. But, this is not exactly for tourists.

It's ok, I said. I know someone there.

OK, but be careful my friend.

I might need to stay, I told him. You know anywhere cheap? Friendly?

He went out the back and came back with my car keys (a Honda Civic) and a business card for a guest house.

They will have a room for you, he said.

That's very kind of you, young man. He smiled as I gave him what I hoped was a generous tip, and the next thing I was driving away from Mexico City.

Travelling out of the city I was sweating, you should've seen it, disgusting. The fucking roads seemed there to eat me. I must have got lost and readjusted the sat nav in that Honda Civic about a hundred times, but I found the place. Every house, every building here is different, but they all look the same. Where Stevie died – it was a sad place. A villa.

There were no police there. Whatever circus there had been for Stevie had moved on now. The DO NOT CROSS tape sagged dusty in the breeze. No sign of the police. I sat in my rented car across the street for a few hours. Nobody came or went. I got out and went up to the windows to peer

---

17 The teenager had a leopard print tail from a costume shop. His briefcase was encrusted with rhinestones.

in. I couldn't see anything. It looked faintly grand in there. A lot of timber, box files, leather-bound books. Like a judge or something lived there.

The kid (reading from the paper) had told me the house was listed on Airbnb – but we couldn't find it on his iPhone. I guess they remove the listing if it happens to be an active crime scene.


So this old lady is in my bedroom telling me to get up, and I do it, I get up ahora ahora and put some clothes on. By now I'm actually really in the mood for some coffee. I follow her through the door, which is actually a plastic folding/collapsing harpsichord affair, coming off the hinges at the top, and I'm in a small kitchen. There's the woman's husband[18] at the little table. A big pot of coffee. A plate of crazy-looking beans the colour of charcoal.

I eat, and ask for water. The woman gives me Evian in a glass bottle. I'm to drink it from the bottle? I ask her.

Both the woman and her husband blink at me.

Sorry, can I have a glass, I try. I know I'm being pushy, but a glass! I need a glass for God's sake or what is the point in any of it.

She gets me a glass, white from soap with calcium stains around the rim. It gives the Evian a chalky feeling, which actually reminds me of the water where I grew up.

---

18 The woman's husband had a disease of the tail that had caused it to wither very badly. His briefcase was made of Spanish leather, and was circular with a fat zip closure.

I try and smile while I eat the black beans. The coffee is delicious. It all seems fine, until the husband's enormous hand lands on mine.

Time to go, he says. He nods to the car park. I look out and see one of those absolutely awful fucking cars. Those cadillac things. It is full of men, and arms hanging out holding weapons. Sunglasses I can see and the blackness of gold and silver teeth. They put on a show out here, I'm thinking. This is next level. I think of us way back when, black mercs and the fucking cold of it. We didn't hang our arms out the window, we sat there wondering if we'd still be alive in an hour, and talking about something normal to make it feel ok. Where we'd watch the football at the weekend, which pub. Whose house. Nobody, fucking absolutely nobody was wearing sunglasses.

I'd rather not go, I say. I can feel the weight in my legs become unbearable. My hands buzz like they're swelling. I feel sick.

The man smiles. The old woman too, she smiles.

I hear the voices of men in my bedroom. *She* must have let them in there, I realise.

I wonder what the fuck I'm doing here. They're going through my stuff. All my power has gone, I realise. Whatever I once was, it's gone. I'm just this pale white-haired eel. I start thinking, counting all the people who will be waiting for me on the other side. Steven is there at the front of the queue, with the magical head of a carp.

My belongings, I manage to say. I need to gather my belongings.

Don't worry – it's taken care of, says the woman. She sounds like my grandma. She knows what's happening and she's reassuring me, like we're organising a trip on the bus.

Time to go, she says again, but no urgency, just to remind me.

My throat is bone dry. My tongue is a cork. I hear them in my room now, zipping up my bags. I'm following the sound of voices out into the sun. There are five of them. Two cars. The rental Honda Civic I drove here in is gone. I look back at the couple who are by the door of the building now, like proud parents.

I'd rather stay, I manage to say. I have business in the village. I'm here on important business, you understand? Many many people will wonder where I am.

Ahorita, the man says. He doesn't believe a word of it.

You can keep the water, says his wife.

~

Alejandro scrunched the emptied bag of habas into a ball and wedged it into the back pocket of his slacks. He felt some residue of grease transfer to the door handle as he opened the door and stepped into the death room.

A drool-soaked tennis ball rolled slowly towards him. Alejandro nudged it with his foot and squinted at it. He looked around the room: a rucked tangle of bedclothes specked all over with dots of coughed-up lung blood – thickening into a long dragmark across a ripped-open Amazon box with a washbag sticking out of it – and on towards a large black

175

slick of matter that spread in a messy oval over most of the floor, like a big raw crater. Bits of tooth studded the darkness. A bottle of Centenario Reposado lay stuck to the mess, the base of it cracked, next to a plastic bottle of bleach squeezed empty at the middle. Duct tape, stuck all over with beard hairs, ringed the nozzle of it.

Alejandro hunkered down and brushed them with his finger, then tutted and got back up, looking back over at the bed. It was easy to see what had happened. As ever, the techs were trying to be too clever – all that standing around, all that training, it made them too imaginative, made them see only flat details, divorced from causality, until they were unable to select from among them. Alejandro thought of himself as being more stupid, and he was proud of it: that ability to look past details, see in a way that organised phenomena into wide sweeps with little bits of story joining them together – but only little bits, or you got too carried away. That's where the stupidity helped again: you had to be impatient enough to look for the joins within the mess, and dense enough not to get artistic with it. His hand stroked his sternum again and he squinted at the scene again. Whoever'd been killed, they'd pulled him out and clonked him over the head with the bottle, then again in the teeth. Then they'd taped an open bottle of bleach to his mouth and made him drink it to the bottom. He must have been a strong guy: he'd pulled the bottle off. But he hadn't been fast enough. The slick of matter had gut lining and all sorts in it. Alejandro heard the door open behind him.

'You weren't lying about the smell,' he said.

'It's serious,' Teresa said. She was holding a clipboard out towards him. An inked sponge rested on top. He dabbed his fingertips on it and placed them on the squares on the sheet, then wiped them off with a tissue from his back pocket. 'You didn't look at the body?'

Alejandro shook his head and said, 'there's enough here.' He flipped through the rest of the sheets on the clipboard: Caucasian male, early forties, muscular build.

He looked at Teresa.

'What?' she said.

'The cop at the gate told me the guy got killed was a teacher or something. Minister's cousin.'

'I don't think so,' Teresa said. 'Body in the bag's a white guy. Well. Pink guy.'

Alejandro squinted at the blood slick on the floor, at the spattered maths books. Then he looked out at the view. A bull dozed by a lake in the wet grass, wet quiffs of hair darkening on his underside. Hilly fields of corn stretched away towards the dark bulk of the volcanoes. At least the guy had died looking at something nice.

'I think whoever killed this guy, they got the wrong guy,' Alejandro said, which felt absurd, because the dead aren't quite themselves anymore and they aren't quite somebody else either, so how can there be a wrong one, a right one, anyone, really.

'Cop downstairs told me about the owner's cousin. Got done for some weirdness with kids.' He gave a nod at the blood spattered maths book. 'Think he was earning money doing extra classes.'

177

Teresa put her hand over her mouth and said, 'oh Jesus.'

Alejandro nodded and said, 'think he couldn't keep himself from – well, you know. And I think a parent hired someone to come after him. And found the guy currently out back.'

'The poor guy,' Teresa said.

'Maybe,' Alejandro said. 'We don't know what was in the post for him, either. Why'd you come all this way on holiday and then go hide in the hills?'

'In such dangerous hills,' Teresa said.

'Right.' Alejandro squinted at the washbag. Something glossy and black was sticking out of the bottom of it. He walked over to it and picked it up. His thumb caught on something and there was a click, and a long string of jabber came shooting out all fast and tinny, in the middle of a story. Alejandro jumped and pressed pause but missed and the recorder jumped out of his hands like it had suddenly become a live fish. The voice kept spooling out. He thought of a jet of high pressure water except instead of water it was a stream of sharp, smashed-up bones. He felt the plates of his skull tighten. He found the pause button after what felt like a long handful of seconds and he heard Teresa sucking her teeth.

'You'll never make goalie with form like that,' she said.

'Was that English?' Alejandro said.

'I think so.'

Alejandro picked the clipboard up from where he'd left it on the floor and ran a finger along the list of articles found with the body. He tapped the page and said, 'British passport.'

'Weird accent. Hurts to listen to,' said Teresa. 'A pain right here.' She rubbed the top of her head. 'Like it was softening the bone.'

'Sorry.'

'Occupational hazard,' said Teresa. 'Occipital, too.'

Alejandro looked at the bar of the voice recorder across his hand. It was so shiny that it looked like a flaw in matter, his hand stopping and restarting either side of a shiny black hole. He scratched his head with his other hand and, without wanting to, found himself looking back at the bits of hair sticking to the tape on the Clorox bottle. He handed the voice recorder across to Teresa and said, 'see what your transcription boys can do with this, would you?'

~

They put me in the boot! You probably call this the trunk. I'm lying there, strips of light visiting me as the lads on the back seats heehaw about, making the leather groan, sounding like they're going to come through and crush me under the metal of the seat. I couldn't see anything, but light angled in from somewhere. I could see my skin. Old, burnt. The Spanish language came at me in muffled hypersensations. I tried to relax into this familiarity of stress, settling it quietly under years of muscle ache. They were fidgeting, nervous with it. Not panicking, nothing like that, but the energy was jumping. I imagined having a son. A little mop of golden hair. I often get this vision, in the dark, when I cannot sleep or get comfortable. A jolly little fellow. My chest aching and his imaginary voice saying pretty words. Calling me Dad. I am too old for sons. I am too old for the dark.

Soon the darkness was complete. The radio was turned on, love songs played without words, bloodless music, stripped down into muffles. The lads in the back seats were calmer now. I heard business-like talk. Calm voices. I had the sense we would be stopping soon. I tried to make a fist. I tried to imagine using my fist, but I've got bones like paper these days. I grew sad. I'm crying in there, but not so you would hear it. I heard one of them put his arm up over the back of the chairs – he'd been doing it on and off the whole journey – and rolled into that feeling like I was being held by my son.

The car rocked to a stop. I heard the doors open, and the suspension ease back as the five heavy bodies eased out of the car. I heard their Spanish in the air now, outside the car. Deciding whether to leave me there or get me out now. I found myself running through the checklist. Mother, God, Michelle my sister, the blessing of life, the ability to stand beside a window in the time I have had and exhale, to breathe out. To shout. I am so lucky. I have had a good life. Soon, perhaps, I will have another one. They'll give me children, and a steady place to stand and watch them making things. I don't know. The list has become loose. I honestly do not want to die. I can't believe I have come to fucking Mexico.

Three things happened then:

I saw your face.

The door of the trunk opened.

The street caught fire.

I didn't hear it click, and I didn't see who opened it, but the world came blaring back in. The air was filled with pops of gunfire. I felt the car rock with it. One of the lads who had taken me from the motel appeared above me, he was grinning and thin red tracks lined each of his teeth. This happens when you know you might die, but before that, you want to kill, and the gums bleed. He was holding his two silver pistolas. I realised that he was kneeling at the back of the car, sheltering.

Our eyes met, and I think I distracted him because he lost that smooth motion you need when returning fire. He came out of cover in a bad rhythm, I saw him take two bullets in his chest. He had tried to shoot back, but it was useless. His gums were bleeding more than ever. On his heart, two blooms, a double poppy as he fell sideways along the floor beneath me. He had the neatest hair I have ever seen. His white vest was pristine, but for the blood. I watched him die with my head peeping over out of the boot. I considered reaching for his guns. But I have no interest in firing a gun.

The shooting got worse. I could hear police sirens now. Apart from this boy[19] dying on the floor, I didn't see anything, but there were at least a dozen voices.

It's alright, I said to the boy. He was gurgling now. He had very green eyes. More bullets hit him, and he cried out. His legs now, five, six hits. Making ribbons of his legs. This stopped him.

---

19 The boy dying on the floor had a tail that was fading as blood flow began to slow. It was a thick tail with tough, creased skin like an old man's hands. His briefcase was lime green, plastic with yellow clasps.

They have an energy, the dead. A human body is a frightening structure when no life is left in it. A warm one especially. It taunts you. The energy of softness, the rubberiness of a face that cannot smile. I stared at him for too long. More bullets thudded into the car. And then I saw your face. You were running away, of course. You turned back to look at something. I don't think you realised that you turned back to look at me until we were staring into each other's eyes. I could smell burning then. Black smoke curling up under the lid of the boot. The car was on fire. I was already choking when I unfolded myself out, landing on top of the boy who had just died. His blood soaking instantly into me.

Under the car, through the smoke, I could see more faces – dead gangsters with beautiful hair, staring at me with their cheeks pressed into the grit on the road. Eight eyes, and heads gelled black with molten hair and bone. The smoke scorched me. I rolled back to where you were running away.

I didn't realise until I stood up, and tried to see a place to run to myself, that this had all taken place outside a chicken shop called Santo Gallo. The place was empty, but through the smoke the details flashed out, blood on the tiles, shattered windows. Three cars on fire. A Santo Gallo worker[20] was on their face, red gashes down the neck, clots connecting the red horizontal stripes of the uniform. I didn't see any children. I heard police sirens and ran in the same direction I had seen

20 The Santo Gallo worker had a pale cream leather briefcase, reminiscent of the padded walls of an old sanitorium. Their tail was naked and handsome like a pet rat.

you running – out across what I now saw was a car park. You probably call this a parking lot.

I ran, though my legs were still aching from being hunched in the back of that car. And I'm old. I ran, it jarred to run in the sandals I was wearing, but I ran. I didn't realise how slow I was running until I saw the speed of the heavily built detective sprinting past me like Linford Fucking Christie. His whole body rolled with each stride. His piss-coloured shirt sagged out of him. His gun was drawn, and I realised he was chasing you.

I kicked off the fucking sandals, and though I could feel blood in my lungs from the smoke, I sprinted, barefoot, through the car park, across the freeway, screaming as I heard the screeching of brakes around me, over the barriers, and into the field on the far side of the road.

In the distance I saw light aircraft landing. I saw hangars and wire fences. I saw you, your noble head bobbing ahead in the distance. You look more than ever like a wooden spoon when you are fearing for your life, my friend. Your big startled face. No hair at all at the front – a hair line that runs across your head from the backs of your ears. I couldn't have seen all of this, but I swear I saw it, your transparent eyebrows. A smile hiding in the shock of your mouth. I called your name, but I fell as I called.

At first I thought I had tripped, or my knee had gone, but soon – pretty much as I died, as the breath left me, I realised I too had been cut down. A cop of my own. Hadn't there been the sound of her screaming drop the gun. I swivelled my eyes to see I was holding that boy's silver pistolas after all.

183

One in each hand. I tried to squeeze the trigger, but my spine was gone. She'd switched me off.

There was nothing to do but watch you, hopping about in the long grass, little pops of your gun. Heavier return fire from our police detectives. Your hands, I thought of your hands, pale and strong. I met your father once; a carpenter. He had the same hands. He made my mother a telephone table. They don't have telephone tables anymore, I believe.

I found myself opening my briefcase. I did not realise that I had been carrying it with me all this time, but of course I had. I reached inside and drew out the files I would need.

I began talking. I talked to the ground, I wanted to record it all. As I died. I slipped out of the body and I talked to the stones in the ground. A black stone, I found. A little strip of obsidian – doubtless from one of Mexico's many volcanic deposits. I resolved somehow to get this to you. I have dictated all of it, and somehow it will come to you. And you'll have to listen to it. This. Whatever this is, me doing this. Me talking to you.

I talked and watched them kill you, and wondered if you would slither out of your body too, and come with me – to see what they give us next. If they let us have anything now. If there is anything. I remained still, unable to travel away from the body of myself. And across the grass, like a sea, three shapes, kneeling one at a time, at each of the dead.

~

Back at home, his shirt open behind him in a big sweat-soaked yellow wing, Alejandro dozes on his beige sofa. His tail aches and he feels dust and grit getting into the folds. He dreams of blood. That's OK. That's to be expected. Today was a lot of blood and zero answers. On his way back from the murder scene he got called away towards the airport, where some shooting was happening: an attempted kidnapping, they said on the wires – an idiot checking into the wrong Airbnb and ending up in the trunk of a jeep – nothing to do with the morning's murder, nothing to do with anything. The corners of his eyes feel dusty. He wipes them and tries to tune deeper into the dream: Teresa is telling him when blood browns and blackens in fabric, the blood is still alive for a while. It's a rare day that he knows as much about anything as Teresa knows about everything so he doesn't ask if he hears her right, he just says, 'oh, like Kombucha', and Teresa says yes. The ringing of his phone wakes him. It's a tech guy from forensics.

'You good?' Alejandro says, picking up the phone, getting to his feet.

'Sort of.' The tech guy's voice sounds shaky. 'It's this voice. It's destroying me.'

Alejandro looks around the room: the kitchen island, the framed photos of canyons and sunsets. He sees small pinholes of black open in them like coughed-up dots of lung blood.

'Go on,' he says.

'I hooked the recorder up to the computer,' the tech guy said. 'And the speakers started screaming. And the air filled with this horrible smell.'

185

'Like fish soup,' Alejandro said, rubbing his forehead.

'Yeah, just like that. And I couldn't tell where it was coming from. I checked the microwave. I checked the bins. I opened a window. And then I went back to the computer and the smell was coming out of the speakers at the same time as the screaming.'

Alejandro is walking around his kitchen. He comes to a stop. He hears his slippers scrape on the grouting between two tiles.

'A sound had a smell,' he says.

'Yes,' says the tech guy. 'Awful. It was like every part inside the speakers and the computer and the recorder was wrenching against every other part, giving off this burning fish soup smell. I couldn't stay in the room. I left. I put on headphones. I could still smell the smell.' Alejandro hears him clear his throat and swallow. 'I got sick a couple of times and I can still taste it. Feel like everything's turning into that smell, into that scream.'

Alejandro doesn't want to turn his head. He feels sure that there is a slick of dark matter in his peripheral vision but when he turns to look for it there isn't one.

'I feel like it's burning holes in my brain,' the tech guy says. 'And that smell is the holes opening up in my brain.'

'Is it all printed out?'

'I went back into the room and checked and yeah, it's all done. Printed out. The smell's still there too.'

Alejandro listens to the tech guy and he squints through the floor-to-ceiling plate glass window: palm trees bobbing their heads in the powdery lilac dusk. Malls, towers, and car bonnets glint in the last of the light.

He thinks about the printout that will be waiting on his desk when he goes to the office tonight, and he feels dread roll like a billiard ball up and down and around the wall of his stomach. He thinks of the white gaps between the lines of typed-out transcript as a maze of snow that he might not be able to get out of, reading at the centre of a smell that won't go away, as though he's trapped inside the body of God and that's just what it smells like in there, inside that God rotting on the beach where he's lain since the seventh day of creation. Alejandro rubs a hand up and down his sternum and tries to bring himself back into his body.

'I'm sorry I did that to you,' Alejandro says. 'I'm sorry. I didn't want to do that to you.' But the tech guy has already hung up, and he's talking to the pulsing of a tone. He can feel the smell wafting out of the speaker at the bottom of his phone, tapering up in fine pale threads.

# Contributors

**Leila Aboulela** is the first-ever winner of the Caine Prize for African Writing. She is the author of six novels: *River Spirit, Bird Summons, The Kindness of Enemies, Minaret, The Translator* and *Lyrics Alley*, Fiction Winner of the Scottish Book Awards. Her short story collection *Elsewhere, Home*, won the Saltire Fiction Book of the Year. Leila's work has been translated into fifteen languages and she was long-listed three times for the Orange Prize (now the Women's Prize for Fiction). Leila grew up in Sudan and now lives in Scotland.

**Roelof Bakker** is a Hastings-based artist/writer and the publisher of Negative Press London. Recent writing has appeared in the anthologies *Responses to Derek Jarman's Blue (1993), Responses to Pale Blue Dot (1990) by Voyager 1* and *Responses to Love's Work (1993) by Gillian Rose* (all Pilot Press, London, 2022), as well as in multiple editions of *Unthology* (Unthank Books, Norwich) and *Confingo* magazine (Confingo, Manchester). His latest book is *Some Queer Animals* (Negative Press London, 2023).

**Ruby Cowling** grew up in Bradford and lives in London. Her short fiction has won *The White Review* Short Story Prize and the London Short Story Prize among other awards. Her collection *This Paradise* (Boiler House Press, 2019) was longlisted for the 2020 Orwell Prize for Political Fiction and shortlisted for the 2020 Edge Hill Prize.

**Adrian Duncan** is an Irish writer. His latest novel *The Geometer Lobachevsky* was shortlisted for the Walter Scott Prize, 2023. His next novel *The Gorgeous Inertia of the Earth* will be published in 2025 by Tuskar Rock Press.

**Lucy Durneen**'s poetry, short stories, and non-fiction have been published and commended internationally, in journals including *World Literature Today*, *Hotel Amerika*, *Meniscus*, and *Poetry Ireland*. Her non-fiction has been adapted for broadcast on BBC Radio 4 and listed as a Notable Essay in *Best American Essays 2017*, while her first short story collection, *Wild Gestures*, won Best Short Story Collection at the 2017 Saboteur Awards in London, and was longlisted for the Edge Hill Prize 2018. She lives in Cornwall, UK.

**Zoe Gilbert**'s stories have been published in anthologies and journals worldwide, and won prizes including the Costa Short Story Award 2014. Her first book *Folk* was shortlisted for the Dylan Thomas Prize 2019 and adapted for BBC Radio. Her second novel, *Mischief Acts*, was a Sunday Times Book of the Year in 2022.

**Gurnaik Johal** is a writer from West London. His collection of stories, *We Move*, won a Somerset Maugham Award and the Tata First Book Award. He won the 2021/22 Galley Beggar Press short story prize and was shortlisted for the 2019 Guardian 4th Estate story prize. His first novel is forthcoming from Serpent's Tail.

**Jo Lloyd** has won the BBC National Short Story Award and an O. Henry Prize and her collection, *The Earth, Thy Great Exchequer, Ready Lies* (US title: *Something Wonderful*), was shortlisted for the Edge Hill Short Story Prize. Her stories have appeared in *Zoetrope: All Story*, *Ploughshares*, *Southern Review*, *Best British Short Stories*, and on BBC Radio 4. She grew up in South Wales where she now lives.

**Tim MacGabhann** is an Irish writer who divides his time between the UK, Paris and Mexico City. His first two novels, *Call Him Mine* and *How to Be Nowhere*, were published by Weidenfeld and Nicholson. Other fiction, non-fiction and poetry has also appeared in *The Stinging Fly*, the *Dublin Review*, *The Tangerine*, *Magma*, *Poetry Ireland Review*, and *The Rialto*, among others. He is currently at work on a PhD with funding from CHASE at UEA. A memoir and a full poetry collection are forthcoming in 2025.

**Jarred McGinnis** was chosen as one of the UK's ten best emerging writers. His debut novel – *The Coward* – was selected for BBC 2's *Between the Covers*, BBC Radio 2's *Book Club* and listed for the Barbellion Prize. His short fiction has been commissioned for BBC Radio 4 and appeared in respected journals in the UK, Canada, USA and Ireland.

**Jon McGregor** is the author of five novels and two story collections. He has been longlisted for the Booker prize three times, shortlisted for the Goldsmiths, and has won the Sunday Times Young Writer of the Year Award, the Betty Trask prize, the IMPAC prize, and the Costa Novel of the Year award. He lives in Nottingham.

**Ben Pester**'s debut short story collection *Am I in the Right Place?* was published by Boiler House Press, and was long listed for the 2022 Edge Hill Prize. His work has appeared in *Granta*, *The London Magazine*, *Hotel*, *Five Dials* and elsewhere. When not writing fiction, he is a technical writer. He lives with his family in North London.

**David Rose** was born in 1949. He is the author of two novels – *Vault* and *Meridian* – and two story collections – *Posthumous Stories* and *Interpolated Stories*. He appears in *The Penguin Book of the Contemporary British Short Story* (ed. Hensher).

**Nell Stevens** writes memoir and fiction. Her debut novel, *Briefly, A Delicious Life*, was long listed for the Dylan Thomas Prize and was a *Financial Times* Book of the Year. She is the author of two non-fiction books, *Bleaker House* and *Mrs Gaskell & Me*, which won the 2019 Somerset Maugham Award. Her writing is published in *The New Yorker, The New*

*York Times*, *Vogue*, *The Paris Review*, *New York Review of Books*, *The Guardian*, *Granta* and elsewhere.

**Eley Williams** has work anthologised in *The Penguin Book of the Contemporary British Short Story* (Penguin Classics, 2018) and *Liberating the Canon* (Dostoevsky Wannabe, 2018). Her collection *Attrib.* (Influx Press, 2017) received the James Tait Black Memorial Prize for fiction with new short stories appearing in *Moderate to Poor, Occasionally Good* (4th Estate, 2024).

**Anna Wood** lives in London and is the author of *Yes Yes More More*, a brilliant collection of short stories.

# Notes

**Merrily Merrily Merrily Merrily**
Nell Stevens Copyright © 2024
Eley Williams Copyright © 2024

**A Note by Eley Williams**
Nell and I collaborated once before on a non-fiction essay
[in *Dog Hearted*, Daunt Books, 2023]. We styled it as a
game of 'Fetch' – I sent off a thought which she sent back
as an answer or end to the sentence. It had a nice literal
back-and-forthiness to it.

However, in a short story, narrative requires shaping
and consequence. It was a case of pre-planning; who are
the characters we want here? Do we want this to be like
a conversation? Do we want this to have recognisable
hinge-work to it? Or do we want to fuse together and write
a story where we've almost been editors shaping something
together?

We ended up having a combination of both; Nell
thinks in a particular way which is very useful to me
who doesn't think at all. She worked out that for a

three-thousand word story, we'd each write six sections of five hundred words. She made a text box, filled in her five hundred words and sent it to me. I then sat and wrote 2000 words... In these she saw the shape of something; by cutting and moving it around, what emerged was a set character who is, in one way or another, being haunted by another.

I really value and enjoyed the experience of collaboration – it felt very freeing to have a reason to be writing in a certain way and to have the convivial pressure of being literally answerable for the decisions you make to someone you make a life with. It felt invigorating and enlivening as a process of writing.

## Keep Your Miracles to Yourself

## A Note by Jarred McGinnis

With a preparation of seven hazelnuts and Syrian rue it was possible to create a call and response between the two main characters as we held the story and its narrative direction in our collective mind's eye, intuitively working together though separated in time and space. That was the first draft anyway, then it was a bunch of emails and shared Google docs to refine the text.

**The Girl Chewing Gum**

**A Note by 'the Author'**

One of my favourite film makers is a British artist called John Smith, whose work is at once witty and profound. In 1976 he released *The Girl Chewing Gum*, a 16-minute black-and-white film consisting of footage of a London street. A camera pans and tilts as the world passes in and out of shot and the voice of 'the director' issues instructions. At one point a girl chewing gum is announced. She enters, lingers and leaves the frame. It was this figure we made the central image of our story. Early drafts suggested that the film inspired us in different ways, and for a while the story struggled. It was when we stopped trying to press it into a conformative shape and let it head off along our diverging desire paths that it came together into a whole.

**Morphic Resonance**

**A Note by David Rose**

This story initially linked a long-standing interest in the ideas of Rupert Sheldrake, around Morphic Resonance, with a more recent preoccupation with the Existential problem of happiness – specifically, the burden of happiness, the obligation to preserve those moments of happiness within memory. A chance conversation with Roelof about dementia, and what happens when such memories become irretrievable, led to our collaboration on the project for *Duets* and the resulting text.

**Junction 11**

Gurnaik Johal Copyright © 2024

Jon McGregor Copyright © 2024

**A Note by Jon McGregor**

We came at this project with such an elaborate set of starting points and rules that I can't quite remember how we ended up at 'Junction 11'. There was a list of well-known duets (Sonny and Cher; Dusty Springfield and the Pet Shop Boys; Freddie Mercury and David Bowie...), some kind of randomised selection of lyrics, and an agreement to start and finish each leg of the journey on the same lyric. We swapped steering wheels a couple of times, and shouted suggestions from each other's back seats. We were stuck in the services for a long time, but in the end we got back on the open road.

**The Backyard of Fuck Around and Find Out**

Ruby Cowling Copyright © 2024

Anna Wood Copyright © 2024

## A Note by Anna Cowling/ Ruby Wood

We cannot speak as individual writers; our souls are now irrevocably merged as a result of this process. JL Borges and C Rooney sometimes make an appearance too. We drink great coffee.

## The Grief Hour

## A Note by Leila Aboulela

Lucy and I each worked on a separate fictional character and although the two never come face to face in the story, they are connected by place and theme. The trigger was a photo Lucy sent me. Looking back, I am surprised at how little time we spent planning or discussing the story. We relied more on reading and responding to each other's segments.

## Apricots

## A Note by Tim MacGabhann

I've this self-contained thing going with the novels and the poems (which are written by a guy from the novels), and the satellites of those novels end up as my short stories – the lives of the 'minor' (nonsense word) 'characters' (nonsense category).

And ultimately, too, the fiction is just a *Lady from Shanghai* hall-of-mirrors thing as relates to the nonfiction I write.

It can get weird/ airless/ laugh-free in there and so it was a real rescue mission from Ben, whose work has such warmth, daring, and mercilessness all at the same time, to come in there with me. He can put a voice on characters like a pressure hose shooting only ceramic shards – what that does to my sense of reality is the most refreshing scathe. Reading him helps me remember what people are like. I don't know how he does what he does. I also don't know how it was for him having me come into his world or whatever, or indeed if even if that's what the experience of collaborating was for him, but I will say that it was such a relief and an honour to put this together with the main man.

**A Note by Ben Pester**
The Mexico of Tim's literature is about as serious as it gets, and his broader work that continues the (often border-line impossible) lives of these characters is a symptom of the unbending humanity found in his writing. They leave the page in one form and stroll onto another page unchanged, but faced with new trials. They are indefatigable, changed but never broken. The connection I have always seen in Tim's work between the fictional and the biographic is that whatever is happening, these impulses, these lives, cannot help but go on, any more than the writer can stop memory pouring through, or the rain from spreading across the streets, or the sun from shining. It was a sacred thing to be allowed to walk around in that world.

On the process, we pretty much agreed that it would be fun to try a sort of call-and-response thing in the writing. It begins with a correspondence and a certain amount of 'make believe' letters between us both.

Pretty soon though, we were just writing a story together. The artifice of writing to each other 'in character' was not needed beyond the initial larks of trying it out.

Since then it felt natural to play it out like a police procedural. You see one side, then the other, and the fact that the mystery of whatever is going on never gets resolved is both a facet of the pointlessness of trying to be a crime fighter whilst living inside of crime itself, and of trying to be a gangster when you're just an old man with bigoted views and a disappointing life to look back on.

We were also not completely unaware that we were writing *HEAT* (Mann, Thomas 1995) for the salted caramel generation.